Jean Ure

£1.99
J

Jean Ure lives in a three-hundred year old house in Croydon with her husband and a family of rescued animals (seven dogs, four cats). She trained as an actress but writing is the only real job she has ever had – her first book was published while she was still at school. She is a vegan and a committed animal rights worker.

Also by Jean Ure

Plague
Watchers at the Shrine

for younger readers

Brenda the Bold

Contents

Jean Ure
After the Plague

Previously published as *Come Lucky April*

mammoth

First published in Great Britain 1992
by Methuen Children's Books Ltd
as *Come Lucky April*
Published 1993 by Teens · Mandarin
Published 1995 by Mammoth
Reissued 1999 by Mammoth
an imprint of Egmont Children's Books Limited
239 Kensington High Street, London W8 6SA

ISBN 0 7497 2711 X

1 3 5 7 9 10 8 6 4 2

A CIP catalogue record for this title
is available from the British Library

Printed in Great Britain
by Cox & Wyman Ltd, Reading, Berkshire

To Miriam,
who fought me womanfully
every inch of the way

Chapter One

*CROYDON COMMUNITY CENTENARY
PAPER: APRIL HARRIET*
*Exactly one hundred years ago there
was a great plague which devastated
civilisation as it was then known. The
origins of this plague have never been
discovered but it is thought it may have
been man-made and released upon the
world by accident.*
*If you should ask how such a thing
could come about—*

April paused and nibbled reflectively at the top
of her pen. As usual she had managed to splat-
ter ink all over herself. In the olden days,
apparently, they had had pens which would
write without having to be constantly dipped
into ink wells, but the supply had run out many
years before April was born. They must have
been a boon.

She sighed, and pushed ink-splodged fingers
through her curls. April was not in the least
academic. If you asked her, this business of
writing papers for the centenary exhibition
would have been better left to those who enjoyed
it and were good at it, such as Meta,
industriously scribbling away on her side of the
room. Of course it had been Rowan's idea.
Rowan was the community's unofficial
historian. (She was also Meta's mother).

'*If you should ask how such a thing could come about* –' resigned, she dipped her pen back into the ink pot –

the world as it then was was divided into many different nations, or tribes, for the purposes of fighting. Many of these nations (called 'the Advanced Nations') had vast stockpiles of weapons. There were:
1) Conventional weapons (swords, guns, etc.)
2) Nuclear weapons (hydrogen bombs, rockets, etc.)
3) Chemical weapons (defoliants, etc.)
4) Bacterilogical –

April broke off and gnawed again at her pen.

4) Bacteriological weapons (plague, etc.)
All nations had governments, which were in charge of the people and told them what to do. The governments were mostly made up of men, because before the plague the order of society was reversed and it was men who were the dominant sex. They were aggressive and liked fighting, hence all the weapons. Men would still be aggressive today if it were not for their training. In those days they were not trained and roamed the world in hordes, murdering and killing and causing havoc. Women could not walk outside without being molested and were scared to emerge during hours of darkness. Every day there were reports of women being raped or mutilated, sometimes even in their own homes. Nothing was done to prevent it on account of the governments being mostly

men. It was the governments who arranged for the wars.

At the time of the plague none of the Advanced Nations was engaged in a war as they were too worried about the world coming to an end by reason of pollution. (Pollution was caused by technology, e.g., aeroplanes, motor-cars, nuclear power stations, etc., which poisoned all the seas and the rivers, killing the trees and the flowers, making holes in the atmosphere, etc.)

So where did the plague come from? This is a mystery which has never been solved. People who were religious, i.e., holding primitive beliefs and worshipping idols, etc., said that it was a punishment on mankind for all the things they had done to the earth. (They did not say it was a punishment on womankind. This was because men were the rulers and women had to suffer for their sins.)

Whatever it was and wherever it came from, it spread rapidly throughout the world until within months there were only a very few people who had been spared. Once upon a time the population of the earth could be counted in millions, if not billions, but after the plague it was maybe only a few thousand, scattered about the globe. It is impossible to be accurate as the means of communication which were there before the plague, when people could talk to each other across the world with an instrument called the telephone, are now lost to us.

However, the fact that the world fell silent and that there has been no attempt, so far as *we know, to restore civilisation as it once was, would seem to indicate that there now exist only a very few isolated communities, such as ourselves. It may be that one day people will begin to reach out again and explore, and links will be established, but for the moment it is thought that distances between communities are too great, and communities themselves too small, for this to happen.*

In the centenary museum will be artefacts from the past, such as: telephone, television, machinery –

At this point April broke off again and sat for several minutes gazing through the window. The sun was shining and she had a sudden itch to be outside in the open air instead of stuffing here indoors, labouring over an essay. She glanced across at Meta, still hunched at her desk, long black hair hooked behind her ears, hand racing busily to and fro across the page.

'If we had an early middy,' said April, 'we could go scavving.'

'Mm?' Meta slowly raised her head.

'I said,' said April, 'that if we had an early middy we could go scavving.'

'Mm . . . I suppose.'

'We ought to do it while the weather's good.'

Scavving – short for scavenging, officially known as searching for artefacts – was no fun in the rain. Early generations had done a clean sweep of both the immediate and outlying areas while roads and property were still in good repair, bringing back all usable and non-perishable articles for long-term storage. These days it was a question of foraging, of hacking

4

one's way through tangles of vegetation and clambering at one's peril over piles of rubble, which April did for the excitement of it and Meta for what she called 'the historical perspective'. April, to be honest, wasn't too struck on history. It seemed to her that the past was either a storehouse of delights which had been lost to them, in which case why dwell on it, or a place of barbarous atrocity and almost unbelievable squalor which they were well rid of. Either way, as far as April was concerned, there was more than enough living to be done in the present.

She flung her pen on to her desk – scattering more blobs of ink – pushed back her chair and went over to Meta.

'Heavens! You've practically written a book!'

She picked up the first page, covered in Meta's neat hand.

'"Croydon Community Centenary Paper: Meta Pauline. The Croydon Community was founded a hundred years ago by a small group of people who had survived the terrible plague of August and September. One of the founding members, who had great influence on the way the community developed, was a woman doctor, Dr Alison" – oh! wailed April. 'I haven't even mentioned Alison!'

'That's all right.' Meta took the page from her and calmly clipped it with the rest. 'We don't all have to write the same thing. We've each got to put what seems most important to us.' She slid her papers away in her desk. 'Where were you thinking of going?'

'Down to have middy!'

"Yes, but after middy?"

'I thought we'd try somewhere new –

5

somewhere no one's been for ages.'

'If there is anywhere.'

'Of course there is! Some places haven't been scavved for years. We'll look on the map.'

The map was kept in the central hall of the main house, where the refectory was. It covered almost the whole of one wall and took in several miles of the surrounding countryside. Coloured flags were dotted about it, clustered thickly in the centre, fanning out towards the edges. The flags were coloured according to decade; every flag was also numbered. In a large book, kept on a desk at one end of the hall, you could check, using colour and number, what the status of any given area had been at the time of the last search – see whether it had been considered worth a future visit or whether there were any special hazards to watch for.

The very earliest flags, dating from Year 2 after the plague when the system had been started, were by now a faded red. There were more of these than anything else, mostly in the central areas.

'Look for blue,' said Meta. 'Blue or green. They're your best bet.'

Blue and green had been used at the time of greatest exploration, between the post plague years 10 to 30, when the community had felt sufficiently established to put out feelers and roam further afield. Since then, as the old road system had broken down and properties gradually became derelict, the outlying areas had been much visited. There was always the chance of uncovering something which previous generations had overlooked.

'How about here?' April jabbed a finger on the map.

Meta shook her head. 'Too far. We'd need a

whole day. This looks better.' She pointed to a small gathering of blue and yellow flags, almost due south. 'It doesn't look as if anyone has been there since the sixties, and only once before then.'

'All right. Go and check it out and I'll work out how to get there.'

Meta went off, obediently. She might be strong on history, but she had absolutely no sense of direction. It was always April who had to plan the route. By the time Meta came back, to announce that in '25 a foraging party had combed the area, and that in '62 another brief visit had been paid but not much of any value uncovered, she had a route firmly fixed in her mind.

'I suppose it is worth the effort?' Meta sounded suddenly doubtful.

'Of course it is! There's always something to be found. It's a question of looking properly.'

'Well, I've written us in.' Meta leaned forward and stuck a purple flag next to the blue and yellow ones.

In a community which prided itself on the minimum of rules and regulations, the rule of 'writing in' was strictly enforced. Scavving was a popular pastime amongst the younger members of the community, but it could also be a dangerous one. Back in the early years of the century one of the founder members, April's great-grandmother Harriet, in fact, had broken the rule and gone off by herself without letting anyone know. It had been almost a decade before her remains had been found. Meta sometimes accused April of taking after her.

'I don't know about Come Lucky,' she would

grumble – 'Come Lucky April' being April's full name, as it was recorded on the official register – 'more like happy-go-lucky, if you ask me.'

Some thought them an ill-matched pair, serious studious Meta and happy-go-lucky April, but they had been friends since infancy and had shared a room since entering the girls' house at the age of eleven. April couldn't imagine wanting to be close, not really close, with anyone save Meta. Cynics might laugh and shake their heads, but sometimes couples did stay together. You only had to look at Willow and Rowan: they had started off by sharing a room in the girls' house and were sharing still, thirty years later.

'We shall be like that,' thought April.

It was early for the midday meal and only a few of the tables in the refectory were occupied. John, behind the counter, was still laying out the last of the dishes.

'What's on?' April peered distastefully at a large pot of something green and dark and glistening. 'Ugh!' Not barley and watercress soup *again*. 'It looks like duck slime!'

John smacked at her with his soup ladle. There was no love lost between him and April.

'You just think yourself lucky! There's some as would be only too grateful for this.'

'Oh, yes?' said April. 'Where?'

'Somewhere.'

'Somewhere nowhere!'

If other communities still existed April felt pretty certain they would have better things to eat than barley and watercress soup. 'Look at it! It's disgusting!'

John, affronted, said: 'That soup's got a lot of goodness in it.'

8

'Why does goodness always have to be such a revolting colour?'

John's round smooth face turned slowly pink. Meta, hastening to make amends, said, 'I'm going to have some.'

'You're welcome,' said April. Pointedly she helped herself to a glass of water, some rolls and an apple and walked off across the room to join Holly and Linden.

'No soup?' said Holly.

'You jest!' said April.

'Foul, isn't it?'

'That's no reason – ' Meta had arrived, bearing a bowl of green slime and a hunk of bread – 'to be unpleasant about it.'

'I should have said,' retorted April, 'that it was every reason.'

'Well, it's not. Poor old John can't help it. He does his best – and it *does* have lots of goodness.'

April tossed her head. 'I don't like goodness! And I don't like John.'

April didn't like men at all. She said there was something creepy about them.

'All soft and squidgy . . . they turn me up.'

Meta shrugged. Men were just men; she didn't take much notice of them. You all played together when you were little, then the boys were sent off and you didn't see them again for years and by the time they reappeared you'd more or less forgotten about them. Even after they came back they tended to keep themselves to themselves, which seemed to Meta only natural. She could never understand, reading old books, how men and women could have paired off and lived together. What would they have had in common? What would they have found to talk about? And come to think of it, how had there been enough men to go round? Of course one had to remember there had been far more of them in those days. The world, it sometimes seemed to Meta, must have been overrun by them; at least, that was the way it came across in ancient history books. History was always about men. A strange and wasteful arrangement, to have had so many of them, when a few were all that was needed. No wonder the world had nearly destroyed itself. It must have been a hideous place.

'Why are you having middy so early?' said Linden.

'We're going scavving.' Bravely, Meta swallowed the last of her duck slime. 'Want to come?'

April kicked at her under the table. She didn't want Holly and Linden tagging along. Holly was all right, though a bit of a ninny. Her one aim was to start having babies as soon as possible – 'I just love babies!' The community certainly needed babies, but not at the expense of personal development. Being a breeding machine was not exactly encouraged. The trouble with Holly was that she didn't need any encouragement. And the trouble with Linden . . .

To be honest, there wasn't any trouble with Linden. It was just that she made April feel inferior. Lin Alison was some kind of genius. She was also pretty. She was also rather remote and unapproachable, except that Meta seemed able to approach her. She and Linden sometimes spent whole days together, poring over old books. If the truth were known, thought April, savagely biting into her apple, I am jealous. That is horrible horrible horrible and I hate me.

To her relief, just as she had made a decision

10

to stop being horrible and make an effort to be pleasant, she heard Linden explain that she couldn't come scavving because she had some reading to catch up on.

'But Holly could go with you. Do you want to go with them?'

Holly shook her head and looked slightly sulky. April guessed they had had another of their tiffs. She also guessed that Holly would have come if Linden had. Talk about a mismatch! Thank goodness she and Meta didn't row like that.

'I really cannot imagine,' said Meta, as she and April left the refectory together, 'what Lin sees in that girl.'

'I really can't imagine,' retorted April, 'what Holly sees in her . . . she thinks about nothing but books.'

'Holly thinks about nothing full stop, unless it's having babies.'

'At least we *need* babies.'

'We need scholars, too,' said Meta. 'If it weren't for women like Alison we'd have lapsed into barbarism.'

'Alison was a doctor. That's *practical*.'

'Yes, but she encouraged people to go on learning. We cannot live,' said Meta, 'by bread alone.'

'No, and we can't live by duck slime, either! Yeugh! I don't know how you got it down you.'

'Willpower,' said Meta. 'I hope you've remembered where we're going, by the way, because I haven't the foggiest idea.'

'Just listen to yourself!' said April. 'Where would you intellectuals be without us lower grade morons to lead you around? Totally lost, that's where!'

Chapter Two

Daniel paused, to refill one of his empty water bottles from a stream which bubbled down the centre of the road and to consult his street atlas.

He handled the street atlas carefully. It was very old. On the front cover, in letters so faded he could only just make them out, it said, 'London A–Z de luxe Street Atlas and Index'. On the back was some kind of diagram, marked 'Underground £3.95'. He had puzzled for a long time over that, trying to work out what it could have been. It was a system of lines and circles, with what he assumed were place names written at regular intervals. He was able to decipher South Kensingtun (?) and Green Park and one or two others, but mostly they were too scuffed and scratched to be legible.

Inside, the street atlas had – or had had, a large swathe was missing – 225 pages. One hundred of these pages were headed 'Index to Streets'. All the rest were maps of different parts of London. He had never realised before how vast it must have been.

It was Philip who had found the street atlas. He had given it to Daniel shortly before he died.

'Here,' he had said. 'You'll need this, for the Quest.'

Philip had often talked about the Quest, how one day he and Daniel were going to strike out on their own, sail round the coast and up the Thames to London, then due south, on foot, to find the Diary. Daniel had never been quite sure that he really believed in it, until Philip had gone and he had been left with the street atlas. After that, it had come to seem almost a sacred duty. He would have felt he had failed his brother's memory if he had not made use of the precious gift he had bequeathed him. In any case, with Philip gone a restlessness had come over him. There *was* a world out there, if only he had the courage to go and look for it.

His mother, he knew, had been reluctant to part with him. That was understandable. With a husband scarcely twelve months dead and an elder son still warm in his grave, she feared to lose the younger one. He felt for her; but he was determined on going. Besides, she still had Ricky and the girls. Ricky was too small, as yet, to be of much protection, but the girls were grown. They would keep her company. He had tried his best to comfort her with this, but she had only shaken her head and said, 'If you have the spirit in you, then you must go where it takes you,' as if already she were resigned to never seeing him again. She hadn't said as much, but he knew she was pinning her hopes on the Council refusing him permission. As it happened, they had not only given him permission – though he would have gone even without it – but had given him their blessing, and helped kit him out for the journey.

He had strict instructions, if he came upon other communities to run no risks: 'Make no attempt to fraternise. Note their position, but avoid contact wherever possible'.

It was assumed automatically that other communities would be hostile. The great plague had had a devastating effect not only on people but on animal life and crops. For decades large tracts of land had proved stubbornly infertile. Grass had grown in abundance; weeds had flourished and run out of control. Crops, for some reason, had failed persistently year after year. Even now, a century later, it was sometimes touch and go. In a situation where food, if not exactly in short supply, was at any rate a precious commodity to be guarded, then, so the Council's argument ran, you could expect trouble. At any rate, it was as well to be on your guard.

To that end they had furnished him with weapons – a pistol, for self-defence, a rifle, for shooting game – and a supply of ammunition. What they had looked for in return was news of an outside world where no one had ventured for decades, or at any rate not come back to tell the tale. Certainly to Daniel's knowledge no one had ever planned on going as far as London. A few miles round the coast, perhaps – a party back in the sixties had reached the old port of Southampton and reported it derelict – but London might as well have been the moon for all anyone ever seriously thought of going there, though once upon a long time ago men *had* set foot on the moon, so legend had it.

Was it legend? Or was it fact? You could read about it in old books – not that Daniel ever had, not being a great one for reading – but how could you be sure that books were telling the truth? Men made up stories even now to entertain. One of the best tales just lately had been Robbie Miller describing in minute detail how he had visited the continent called America and seen 'buildings as tall as the sky'. Everyone knew he had taken it from an old book, but it made it none the less fascinating. Daniel guessed, reluctantly, that men on the moon was just another made-up story.

The Quest, however, was for real. When he got back and told them how he had sailed round the coast, past all the places that were on the ancient maps – Portsmouth, Hastings, Dover – right round and up the Thames to London; when he told them how he had sailed under Tower Bridge and actually seen the Tower, still standing, where (so they said) it had stood for a thousand years – how he had sailed on, past huge ivy-clad buildings on either side of the river until he reached the next bridge, which his street atlas had told him was London Bridge – how he had tied up the dinghy and set off due south on foot, with never a sign of human life, nor very much more of animal: when he stood up and told them all that, they would know it had not come out of any book but was indeed the very journey he had taken. Philip would be proud of him! And prouder still if he fulfilled the purpose of the Quest and returned in triumph with the Diary.

Thus far, though the journey had been long, and sometimes arduous, and sometimes almost unbearably lonely – Patty had been desperate to accompany him, but a girl's place was at home, and besides his mother had need of her – thus far at least it had proved straightforward. Philip had carefully marked the route for him in his street atlas, and the route that he had marked had been along the large roads labelled 'A' roads on page 12 of the atlas, where it said 'Reference'.

These, presumably, had been the big important roads where people had gone about their business and driven in their moving vehicles. Daniel knew, from the stories that were told, that before the plague there had been constant coming and going, not only over the land but across the sea and in the air as well. His mother always said, what had been the point of it? She could never understand what would have driven folks to want to leave the comfort of their homes and go travelling. Where would they have travelled to? And for what purpose? There were perils enough in life, what with brawls and accidents and storms at sea (she spoke from recent bitter experience) without going out and looking for them. Daniel had no answer for her, yet felt instinctively there was more to life than could be found on a man's own doorstep. The Council, made up of men, who were by nature bolder and more adventurous than women, obviously agreed with him. There had been hints that if Daniel returned safely they might even mount a full expedition.

But that was for the future. For the present – he concentrated on his street atlas, trying to work out exactly where he was. He had gone through the place called Croydon and must now, he thought, be approaching the difficult part, where he had to leave the large roads labelled 'A' and move into the smaller and less important roads, the ones labelled 'B'. Whereas the 'A' roads were still clearly delineated, even though buildings had occasionally crumbled into vast mounds of rubble, and grass had grown up through the artificial covering that had been laid, the 'B' roads had almost disappeared. Many of them had been so completely overgrown that they lay, impassable without the necessary cutting implements, behind thick tangles of thorn and bramble. Others could still be made out, but almost always the names, which, he had discovered, were either on metal plates at the sides of the roads or on plates fixed to the sides of buildings, had become hidden behind giant trees and bushes, all, at this time of year, in full foliage.

Obviously what he must do was decide his exact position then count the number of roads before he had to turn off. He managed at last, by scraping and scrabbling at a large pink bush with rather unpleasant prickles, to uncover part of a name plate: -ling Close. He consulted his street atlas – he was proud of the way he had so quickly become an expert on its usage. He was on page 124, in the bottom left-hand corner. (Pages 122 and 125 were both amongst the sections that were missing. He felt the hand of providence: no part of his journey had lain on these pages. If it had, the whole Quest would have been in jeopardy. He could never have managed it without the street atlas.)

Daniel traced his finger along the 'A' road called Brighton Road until he found what he was looking for – Haling Close. He traced his way on past a further five roads and came at last to the one up which Philip had drawn his red marker line: Whitgift Hill. The red marker went up Whitgift Hill, turned left at the third turning, turned left again and came to a stop. That was it! His destination. Raglan Court, where his great-grandmother had lived until the time of the plague. It was from there that she had set out on her long journey to Cornwall along with her friend Shahid Khan, who had become Daniel's great-grandfather.

Why she had left home was never fully explained in the Journal which she had kept during that worst of times, and which had been handed down through the generations, but a careful reading gave clues. Her parents, she revealed, had both died in the plague. She seemed to have been an only child, and had possibly been trying to reach her grandmother, who lived in the West Country. She had certainly reached the West Country, but whether she had ever found her grandmother was not known, since the Journal finished on what she called 'the 22nd day', at which point she had still been in London.

His elder sister Clemency, as a child, had known the journal off by heart. She had woven endless fantasies round the journey of their great-grandparents from Croydon to Cornwall. The very name 'Croydon' had for her had a magical ring to it. Daniel, as a boy, had been largely indifferent. He had only come to it later, when the possibility of the Quest had roused his interest. Clem, in her eagerness to be involved, had made him a copy 'to carry with you', though by now, like her, he knew great chunks of it by heart.

This is the journal of me, Frances Latimer. I am starting it on Day 1 of the Plague Year. Day 1 because this is the day on which I have decided to keep a record of what is happening. Plague Year because that is how I think of it. If there is anyone who would like to know who I am and what happened to me before this date they can find out from the diary which I kept when I was at home. Home was no. 10 Raglan Court, South

Croydon, in Surrey, and the diary was in the cupboard by the side of my bed. It says 'Private' on the cover but whoever finds it has my full permission to read it. I think by then it will be an historic document.

It was Clem, mainly, who was eager for him to find the Diary and bring it back. For Daniel – as, he suspected, for Philip, and even for Patty– the Diary was merely the spur to adventure. There were enough accounts of life before the plague without coming all this way for yet another. But it gave purpose to the journey, and for Clem's sake he would do his utmost not to return empty-handed.

Counting carefully, he reached the hill where he had to turn off. The surface had grassed over, and the usual thicket of briars and brambles was encroaching from either side, but still there was a path clear up the centre – made, he would guess, by animals, and indeed even as the thought formulated itself a rabbit, or possibly a rat, shot out of the undergrowth and raced across his field of vision. Instinctively he took aim, but it had vanished before he could pull the trigger. Tomorrow, he thought, he would have to set about some serious hunting; but for the moment he would make do with the last of what he had in his pack and concentrate his energies on Clem's precious Diary. Once he had that safe, he could relax and look about him.

To his left, as he made his way up the hill, he could see the top half of one of the great towering blocks, made out of some kind of grey stone, of which there had been so many in the 'A' roads. He couldn't make out what purpose they had served. They had windows – windows by the score, all the way up – so obviously whatever had been kept in there had needed light. He thought perhaps they were what had been called churches, where people had gathered together to worship their gods.

Whatever they were, they seemed not to have been very stable. He had had to pick his way over several quite mountainous piles of masonry, where some of them had collapsed and blocked the entire road. One had actually been shedding bits of itself as he passed; another, interestingly, had split right down the middle, exposing the interior. Inside, it had been composed of layers – layer upon layer, right up into the sky. He supposed, assuming he had guessed their function correctly, that the most important worshippers had worshipped in the top layers, with the women and children down at the bottom.

Some of the women back home would have liked to have religion, but the Council had dismissed it as superstition – all very well for our plague-ridden ancestors, but not for us. Patty, who didn't want religion herself but sometimes tended to be a bit uppity in her ideas, had hinted that if women wanted to get together and pray then they should go ahead and do so, and never mind the Council. What right did the Council have to rule their lives? Her mother had told her, sharply, to 'stop all that nonsense'. One or two of the younger ones had supported her, but none of the older women. It was about time, her mother said, that Patty learnt to know her place.

Daniel laughed. Poor Patty! Patience was the least of her virtues. She had been as cross as a hornet when she'd been told she couldn't accompany him. She'd even had the barefaced nerve to go storming into the Council chamber and try arguing her case. Needless to say, they had paid no attention. She would learn; she was only just sixteen.

At the top of the hill he came to the third turning, which was the one he had to take. Trees were growing so thickly on the crest that for a moment he thought he must have counted wrongly, but looking up he saw the nameplate, Coventry Road, still attached to one of the tall poles with which his ancestors had dotted the landscape. (The poles intrigued him. Some of them were made of wood and had bits of what looked like wire attached to them; he hadn't yet been able to work out what function they could have had. To hang things on? But what?)

He wove a path through the trees, noting to his satisfaction the evidence of wild life, in particular the strong scent of fox and badger. Where there were foxes and badgers, the chances were there would also be rabbits. Tomorrow, he determined, he would eat well.

He very nearly missed the entrance to Raglan Court. A gut feeling that he had gone too far caused him to stop and retrace his steps, peering intently at the ground to his right for signs of what might once have been a road. Even then, he almost didn't see it – the only clue came from a pool of sunlight filtering through a gap in the trees. Investigating, he was just able to discern the faint markings of a path through the jungle of greenery. As he pushed his way through, snagging himself on briars, entangling himself in creepers, the thought occurred to him: he could be the first person to have set foot in Raglan Court for a hundred years . . .

He tried to picture it, how it must have been when his great-grandmother had lived there. The road would have had the hard surface that they put down for the vehicles. There would have been houses, freshly painted, and neat gardens with regimented banks of flowers. He pictured his great-grandmother as a young girl – he pictured her as Patty was now – setting off on foot with Shahid Khan and their friend Harriet, who had never made it as far as Cornwall. He saw the three of them, wearing their masks – he knew from the Journal that everyone had had to wear masks, then and for some time to come – walking, perhaps, on this very spot where he was walking now, and for the first time he felt the thrill of the past and knew why it was that Clem was so anxious for him to find the Diary.

But first he had to find the house. That was not going to be so easy. When he stopped and looked closely he could see that houses were still behind the sprawling mass of plant life, but how was he to tell which numbers they were?

He took out his street atlas again and consulted page 124. Raglan Court was shown as being a very short road. He tried to work out, from the atlas, how many houses there were likely to have been and to pinpoint number 10.

At best it could only be guesswork – but at least he could guess intelligently. He chose a point at what he judged to be the halfway mark, took his axe from his belt and began chopping . . .

He hadn't expected to uncover number 10 at the first attempt; he wasn't looking for that kind of luck. Even when he had hacked and sliced his way through a thicket of unrelenting blackthorn to find the number eleven still attached to the front of a door he didn't necessarily expect number ten to be the next one up. What he did expect, if it wasn't number ten, was that it would at least be number twelve. When he finally managed to reach it and it turned out to be number thirteen, he was thrown into confusion. When he hacked his way back down and uncovered number nine, he was toppled from confusion into rage. What in plague's name had they done with number 10?

He sank down, momentarily exhausted, to consider the matter. Nine, eleven, thirteen . . . use your loaf, Daniel, you dummy! Odd numbers one side, evens the other? (But why? For what purpose?)

Wearily he pulled himself to his feet. He had been on the march since daybreak and reckoned by now that it must be getting on for midday. Leaving his pack, with the rifle strapped across it, he stepped forward with his axe for a fresh assault on the opposite side of the road. The sun bore down on him; the sweat poured, stinging, into his eyes and down the centre of his chest. Maddened, he tore off his shirt, tied a rag round his forehead and carried on. Slash, hack, chop. Slash, hack, chop. Slash, hack, chop.

The rhythm numbed him. He almost didn't register the change of tone when the axe, instead of its normal chump! as it cut through wood, rang out against something metallic. When it finally penetrated his sunbaked skull, he thrust his arm through the gap where he had sent the axe and felt what was either a gate or a fence. Frenziedly he tore aside the encumbering branches of an overgrown beech hedge, entwined with the tendrils of some sort of climbing thing, and found himself staring at the legend 'No hawkers, no circulars'. (Like so much from the past, the words made no sense. He made a mental note to ask Clem.)

By pushing and shoving, he came at last across the number – 10 – inscribed on the gatepost. This was it! The house where his ancestors had lived.

The gate had been left open – a hundred years ago? By his great-grandmother? – but he was able to force his way through and beat a path to the front door, sheltered behind a thick curtain of flowering honeysuckle. Very pretty, he thought, as he tore it down. With the honeysuckle came chunks of rotten timber and a shower of brick dust. Looking up, he saw that a gap had appeared over the door. The door itself, when he kicked it, obligingly fell backwards into the house. Gingerly he stepped after it over the threshold.

Ahead of him was a passage, with doors leading off to the right, and to the left a flight of stairs. He stood for a moment, accustoming his eyes to the gloom of the interior after the raging sunshine outside. He saw the remains of a carpet on the hall floor, and a chest at the far end with a vase standing on it. The place smelt, as was only to be expected, of must and mould, but seemed structurally in reasonable condition.

He walked in, over the fallen door, and across to the stairs. Cautiously he tested the first step: it creaked, but bore his weight. If there is anyone who would like to know who I am and what happened to me . . . Clem would like to know; Clem couldn't wait for him to get back with the precious Diary. The Diary was in a cupboard by

24

the side of Frances Latimer's bed. The bed, presumably, had to be upstairs. There was no way of getting upstairs except by the staircase.

He stood at the foot, looking up, assessing his chances. He put a hand on the rail, half expecting it to crumble at his touch. It didn't.

He tested step number two, waiting for it to collapse beneath him. It didn't.

Holding his breath, he moved up to step number three.

Of course, it was always possible that the Diary would no longer be there. A hundred years was a long time. Anything could have happened to it.

It could have rotted. Been eaten. Gone to dust. Any of those things.

But he owed it to Clem at least to have a try. He couldn't come all this way only to be defeated at the last by his own cowardice. So what if the stairs did collapse? It wasn't that far to fall. The most likely event was that the rail would give way. If he kept to the side, against the wall —

He kept to the side, against the wall. He was almost at the top when, without any warning whatsoever, he found himself plunging downwards in a welter of falling debris.

His last conscious thought, before the darkness closed over him, was for Clem. Now she would never get to see her wretched Diary . . .

Chapter Three

Meta and April collected a couple of scav poles, saddled their ponies and set off down the lane, accompanied as usual by a gaggle of dogs. Dogs, right from the beginning, had attached themselves to the community, drawn by the need for human companionship bred into them over the centuries. Official community history recorded several heated debates amongst the original members on the subject of animal life. There had been a split between those who felt that all animals, including dogs, had but one purpose, to serve humanity; which meant, in the conditions then prevailing, being killed and used as food. On the other hand there had been those who passionately declared that if humanity were to be given a second chance it was essential they stop misusing the planet and everything on it and begin exercising respect and compassion.

It had been Alison, doctor, feminist, and humanist, who had led the debate and whose views had finally prevailed. From that time on, no animal seeking sanctuary within the community had ever been turned away, no animal had ever been abused. No horses put down when too old to be ridden, no chickens slaughtered when they were past laying. A people, Dr Alison had said, should be judged by the way they treated those weaker than themselves.

One by one, as they reached the end of the lane, the dogs peeled off and headed back for home, until they were left with only Shep, a black and white collie type, still young and eager for adventure.

'What we have to do,' said April, 'is ride straight down the hill and across the valley.'

'Then what?'

'Then we take any road going up the other side and that brings us on to Purley Crest.'

'And that's where we're headed?'

'That's the area you picked out.'

'I don't expect we'll find anything.' Meta was always inclined towards pessimism. (She said it was just being realistic.) 'Rowan says by this time most things will have perished.'

'I bet if we went scavving in London we'd find something . . . all those buildings! They can't all have caved in.'

'N-no.' Meta sounded doubtful. Unlike Shep, bounding fleet-footed at their side, Meta really wasn't at all adventurous – at least, not physically. Mentally she was. She couldn't do enough delving into old books. You would have thought, reflected April, that with her passion for history, and with Rowan as a mother, she would be clamouring to be allowed to go and scav round London; Rowan, too. Instead they seemed perfectly content just to read about it in books and look at pictures. Odd, if you asked April.

'I'd give anything to go there,' she said.

'You could always put it up as a suggestion. If you could find enough support – '

'Well, I can't,' said April. 'I've asked, and most people feel like you. I don't know what it is about this place! Anyone would think the

27

outside world didn't exist. Wouldn't you *like* to see all the things you've read about?'

'Well, yes, I *would*,' said Meta.

'But?'

'I suppose – ' Meta gave a little laugh; half ashamed. 'I suppose what it comes down to is that I'm a coward. I don't know what's out there.'

'What could be out there?'

'Anything! I don't know. That's the point.'

'So don't you want to go and see?'

'No,' said Meta. 'But if someone else went, and then came back and told me – '

'That's living at second hand!'

'I know.' Meta hung her head, so that thick black waterfalls of hair gushed down over her shoulders. 'I know it is, and I'm not proud of it, but I told you, I'm a coward. I wouldn't ever do what Harriet did and go out on my own.'

'Well, but that was just stupid!'

'Yes, but it must have taken courage. I don't think I've got any courage, and the worst of it is,' said Meta, 'I don't think I particularly want any. I don't *want* to cross frontiers and blaze trails and put myself to the test. I'm quite happy living like I am.'

'All right,' said April. 'I'll be the one that blazes trails. And then I'll come back and tell you about it, and you can write it down. How about that?'

'I think that sounds like a very good idea,' said Meta.

They reached the bottom of the valley and crossed what had once been the main Brighton Road. Brighton, said Meta unexpectedly, was somewhere she *would* like to go – 'I'd love to see the sea!'

'Yes, well, that isn't practical,' said April, sternly. 'Brighton is too far. The coast is days away. Now, London,' she said, 'you could get to London in only a few *hours*, probably.'

'Unless you got lost.'

'Lost? I wouldn't get lost! Have I ever got lost?'

'Never,' said Meta, humbly. 'Where now?'

'Over there. Up the hill.'

April pointed with her scav pole, which she carried somewhat cavalierly slung over one shoulder. Meta, not quite so sure a horsewoman and needing both hands on the reins, had pushed hers down the side of her pannier, where it stuck up like a lance. April, once, had had the bright idea of fashioning a scav pole that would fold, but hadn't yet worked out a way of doing it.

The sun was hot on their backs as they let the ponies pick their own pace up the hill. Shep hunted ahead of them, in and out of the undergrowth in search of rabbits. He wasn't supposed to be a hunting dog, he was supposed to be a herding dog, but the instinct, perhaps, had been bred out of him. April had once spent hours looking at a dog book in the library. She had been fascinated to see how many different kinds there had been. There were still a few recognisable basic types – terriers, hounds, sheepdogs – but nothing like the variety which had come from selective breeding.

She reflected idly, as she rode, how strange it was that people so advanced as the world had been before the plague should have practised selective breeding on animals but not on themselves. To think that men and women had actually had sex together – had actually *done* things. Or, rather, men had done things. It was

29

the men who did them, the women who had them done. Men who had the pleasure, women all the suffering. She tried, sometimes, to imagine how it must have been, just for the dubious thrill of feeling that faint tingling of revulsion up her spine. Meta said she was mad.

'It must have been dis*gusting*. Why think about it?'

She didn't really know, except that there was an undeniable fascination, occasionally, in thinking about things that were disgusting – so long, of course, as they were safely shut away in the past and not happening now.

Meta's voice broke suddenly into her thoughts: 'Listen!'

'What?'

'*Listen.*'

Obediently, April listened. From some distance away there came the sound of barking. Looking round, she said, 'Shep?'

'He went off through the woods. Is that the way we're supposed to be going?'

'No, we're supposed to be carrying straight on.' April stood up in her stirrups and shouted. '*Shep!*'

He could find his way home, but she wouldn't like to go back without him. Dogs had been known, before now, to disappear down badger setts.

They brought the ponies to a halt and waited. The barking continued.

'He's found something,' said April. 'We'd better go after him.'

'I hope it's not bones,' said Meta.

The dogs even now sometimes came home carrying recognisable parts of human bodies. There had been no question of giving decent burials during the time of the plague; corpses had been left to rot where they lay. Only the immediate area had been cleared, in the interests of hygiene.

'He wouldn't get that excited over a skeleton,' said April.

She set off at a canter, towards the woods at the top of the hill. There was a winding path through the centre, plenty wide enough for a small pony but she had to slow to a walk because of the scav pole, suddenly become unwieldy amongst the trees. Away to her left Shep went on barking, the shrill, imperative bark of a dog who is demanding that someone go and investigate.

'All right, we're coming!' Pressed almost flat against the pony's neck, reins in her left hand, scav pole in her right, April followed the noise to its source. She emerged from the woods on to a narrow track between massed banks of shrubs and bushes. In the middle of the track was Shep, standing guard over what looked to be some kind of bundle with a stick strapped across it.

'What is it?' Meta had appeared at her side.

'I don't know . . . an artefact?'

'But when did it get there?'

'What do you mean, when did it — ' April broke off, as belatedly it struck her, what had struck Meta, the historian, straight away: whatever it was, it could hardly have been lying untouched for a hundred years. Foxes, long since, would have carried it off or torn it apart; either that or it would have rotted.

She dismounted and ran forward.

'It's a bag – with a *gun*!'

'Don't touch it!' Meta screamed the words at her as April, impulsive as ever, was already

31

reaching to pick it up.

'Why not?'

'It might go off!'

April considered it, doubtfully. 'It doesn't look as if it would.'

'You can't tell, you don't know how they work.'

'I do know! You had to press something.' It couldn't hurt just to touch the handle. She was itching to see inside the bag, but it meant moving the gun, and if Meta was going to get hysterical –

'*Shep!*'

April looked up. Now what was the matter? Shep had begun barking again, shrill and urgent as before.

'He's in there,' said Meta. She pointed. Someone, very recently, had hacked passages through the undergrowth. Where Meta was pointing, the passage led to a house, the front door of which was missing. From inside came the sound of Shep's high-pitched barking.

The two girls looked at each other.

'He's found something else,' said April.

'Call him back,' said Meta. 'I don't like it!'

April couldn't decide whether she liked it or not. It was a bit creepy – but it was also exciting. And it wasn't the slightest bit of use calling Shep back because he wouldn't come. The whole point was that they should go to him.

'I'll have to go and get him.'

'Don't step inside!'

'I'm not stupid,' said April, scornfully.

She had been scavving long enough to know that stepping inside was one thing you never did, unless you came properly equipped with an official party. That was what the scav poles were for. In time you became quite expert at hooking things out through doors and windows.

After a second's hesitation Meta dismounted and followed April up the roughly slashed track to the front door – or, rather, the gap where the front door had been. Nervously she peered over April's shoulder. Shep, bright-eyed and moist-nosed, but quiet now that they had obeyed his summons, was eagerly standing to attention over something. In the dim light of the interior, Meta couldn't immediately make out what it was. What she could make out was that the staircase had collapsed, pulling away from the top landing and bringing down half the outside wall. It was exactly the sort of accident they were warned about, as children: never go inside in case the house collapsed on you.

From somewhere amidst the fallen timber and chunks of masonry which marked the spot where the stairs had been there came a sound as of faint moaning. Shep whimpered, and seemed to nuzzle at something.

Slowly, as the two girls watched, a shape rose up out of the rubble. Groaning, it heaved itself into a sitting position. They stared, aghast. The shape was humanoid, yet surely not human? It had dark hair hanging in tangles down to its shoulders, hair over the lower part of its face, hair over its bare chest and arms. It was filthy and bloodstained. It crossed Meta's mind that it was an ape. Apes were not native to this part of the world, she knew that from her reading; but she knew also that in pre-plague days one of the more barbaric practices had been to confine wild animals in cages for the public to stare at, even as they had once stared at the lunatics in a place called Bedlam. Was it possible that at the time of the catastrophe some of these creatures had managed to break free and survive in an alien climate?

Even as she racked her brain in an effort to recall whether the big apes had been considered dangerous, it came to her that no ape, dangerous or not, was likely to walk the country carrying a pack, with a gun strapped to it. It was not an ape. She knew, suddenly, and with chilling certainty, what it was. No ape, but a human being. But such a one as had not been seen in the community for longer than most people now alive could remember. Linnet, perhaps; and Fortune. Certainly not those of Rowan and Willow's generation.

An ignoble urge came over Meta to turn and run. Not that he could do anything to them, injured as he obviously was, and still half buried beneath a pile of rubble, but she felt as she might have felt on coming face to face with a creature from one of the primeval swamps: in the presence of something so unspeakably alien as to curdle the very blood in her veins.

Daniel's immediate impulse, on being brought back to consciousness by the feel of something wet and cold and fringed with fur pushing at his chin, was to reach for his pistol; but his right arm refused to move, and the fingers of his right hand, scrabbling ineffectually at his side, encountered nothing but the leather of his belt. The pistol, it seemed, had gone.

Stiffly, he turned his head towards whatever it was that was pushing at him. A dog. Black and white, with long hair and a plumed tail. Relief at seeing that the tail wagged was tempered almost at once by the reflection that a friendly dog meant a dog that was used to people; and people, as the Council had warned him, were likely to be hostile. Hell and damnation! Where was that pistol?

He tried again to move his right arm, but the pain made him groan aloud. The dog, whiffling excitedly, nuzzled at him with renewed zest. Slowly, Daniel hauled himself upright amongst the rubble. His right arm had been trapped beneath a chunk of masonry; he couldn't be sure whether it was broken or merely bruised. Of the pistol, there was no sign. Grunting, partly with the effort, partly in protest at the discomfort caused to his battered body, he freed his legs from the litter of bricks and timber which pinned them down. The dog licked his face. A voice said, 'Shep!'

Startled, Daniel jerked his head up. Two girls stood in the doorway, looking at him. One was a black girl, tall and slender, with shimmering curtains of hair framing a face of grave, dark-eyed watchfulness. The other, standing in front of her, was shorter and more wiry, with a riot of red curls that blazed like flames in the sunshine. They were staring at him as if he were some creature from outer space; as if they had never seen a man before. He supposed he must look a bit of a sight.

Since he couldn't think of anything to say – he was on their territory: it seemed to him that it was up to them to make the opening remark – he began painfully to hoist himself towards them across the rubble. The black girl instantly retreated. The one with the hair on fire took a step backwards but otherwise stood her ground. The realisation that they were more scared of him than he was of them came as a relief. He had heard tales, before he left, of how previous explorers had fallen into the hands of tribes who had wrenched out their tongues, cut off their hands and feet, pegged them out for the crows to peck at.

April watched as the creature crawled towards her. She was prepared for flight if necessary, but it had not harmed Shep and she could see no reason it should harm her. It looked as if it were in need of help.

Meta had crept back to her side; her fingers curled round April's arm.

'I'm sorry about this,' said Daniel. Meta jumped; so did April. They exchanged glances.

'The stairs collapsed on me.'

If it spcke, thought April, it had to be human. Its voice was strangely deep and gravelly; and the words, though perfectly intelligible, did not have the right sound to them. *They sturs cullopsed on may*. Where had it learnt to speak like that?

April cleared her throat. 'Are you all right?' she said.

'Give or take a broken bone or two.' Daniel tried again to move his right arm. He grimaced. 'It might just be bruising.'

'Is that your pack out there?'

He nodded, preoccupied with feeling for broken bones.

'Have you come far?'

'The West Country.'

'Cornwall?' It was the black girl who spoke.

He said, 'Yes; Cornwall.'

Her eyes flickered over him. He became aware that he had no shirt and that his nether garments were very much the worse for wear.

'How did you get here?'

36

'Sailed round the coast and up the Thames.' Her eyes widened, gratifyingly. 'Then I tied up the boat at London Bridge and walked.'

'*London?*' said the red-haired one. 'You've been in London?'

'Yes. But only – ' he stood upright, and staggered as one of his ankles gave way – 'only the River. I didn't – get a chance – to see – much.'

'You'd better come and sit down.' The smaller girl stepped forward and took his arm. The other wouldn't come near him but stalked ahead to where his pack was still lying as he had left it.

'We didn't touch it.' She gestured towards the rifle. 'What is that for?'

'It's a rifle.'

'I know that; but what is it for?'

'Shooting rabbits, mainly.'

'Shooting *rabbits?*' They stared at him; side by side, accusing.

'Why would you shoot rabbits?' said the redhead.

'Well – ' he sank down, with difficulty, on to the grass. 'It's a long way from the West Country to here. I had to eat from time to time.'

There was a silence.

'You mean,' said the black girl – she said it carefully, obviously anxious not to misread the matter – 'you mean you – eat flesh?'

Didn't everyone? No; he could tell, at a glance, that not everyone did. They had both cringed back from him as if he had confessed to being some sort of cannibal. The black girl looked down at the rifle.

'Is it loaded?' she said.

'Yes, but it's quite safe, it won't go off.'

37

With calm determination she crouched down and began undoing the straps that held it in place. He wanted to ask her, 'What the plague are you up to?' but could only sit and watch, with glazed eyes, as she picked up the rifle by its butt and hurled it savagely into the undergrowth.

'What did you do that for?' said the other girl.

'What do you think I did it for?'

'But it was an artefact!'

'That sort of artefact we can live without.'

'Rowan would say you're not being historically objective.'

'Well, but it wasn't ours, anyway!'

Quite, thought Daniel; it wasn't theirs anyway. He sunk his head into his hands, past caring, for the moment, how – or even if – he was going to survive.

'Can we do something for you?' said the redhead. She took a water bottle from his pack. 'Should you care for a drink?'

They stood watching as he put the bottle to his lips. He had the feeling they would not have been surprised had he poured it into his cupped hand and lapped. What did they think he was? A wild animal? Granted he was in a bit of a mess –

'You had better come back with us,' said the black girl, coolly, 'and let someone look at you.'

He shied away from the suggestion. Dangerous enough to enter an unknown community when you were armed and strong; folly to do so from a position of weakness.

'No one will harm you,' said the girl.

He hesitated.

'Where is your community?'

'Not far.' She turned, for confirmation, to her

companion. 'Say, an hour's ride?'

'About that.'

It was too far. In the state he was in, he would never be able to memorise the route. He needed to be free to make his own way back again. He needed to be free! He wasn't taking the word of two girls no older than Patty that no one would harm him. What did they know about it? They would have no say in the matter. It would be up to the men.

'I'll be all right,' he said, 'when I've rested.'

They regarded him, dubiously. The black girl half shrugged a shoulder; the other, in tones of what sounded to be genuine concern, said, 'But suppose you've broken something?'

'It will mend.' All he wanted was for them to go away, back across their valley and leave him in peace to lick his wounds and assess his chances.

'Have you no clothes?' said the redhead. There was doubt in her voice, now; as if she still was not wholly convinced of his membership of the human race and thought he habitually travelled half naked.

'Yes, I – ' he nodded towards his pack, at the same time casting about for his discarded shirt. He saw it caught on a mass of brambles and make a weak gesture towards it.

'We didn't notice that,' said the redhead, going to fetch it for him. 'If it hadn't been for Shep, we would never have found you.'

The dog lolled its tongue and panted. He supposed he ought to feel grateful but just for the moment he felt too wretched to feel anything very much save an overwhelming desire to be left to lick his wounds in private.

'Did you come here for any special reason?'

That was the black girl again. She was more guarded than the other; more suspicious.

'No, I was just – wandering.'

She raised an eyebrow. He could tell that she didn't believe him, but he couldn't help that. He was too exhausted to make up anything more plausible and he didn't feel inclined to let them into the secret of the Quest.

'What will you do?' said the redhead. 'If we leave you?'

Cunningly he said, 'Oh, I shall lie up and rest for a few days until my strength comes back, then I'll be on my way.'

In fact, he thought, as soon as they had gone he would retrieve his rifle, hopefully his pistol as well, and likewise the axe, lie up for that night ready for one further attempt on the Diary in the morning, and be off and away before they could come for him. He felt certain that they would come for him. He couldn't see any community tolerating a stranger in their area. They would take him in for questioning, if nothing else. Who are you, where have you come from, what are you doing here? It was what he would do in their position. But at least if he could trick these two gullible females into believing he was staying put, it would give him the necessary breathing space.

It was the black girl who was likely to give him problems. The redhead was more concerned with his welfare than with any nefarious intentions he might have. She was considering him now, brows knitted.

'What will you eat?'

He could hardly say rabbit. They obviously belonged to some weird kind of fruit-eating sect that shunned all forms of carnal gratification –

well, all forms except one, though they probably did that with clenched teeth in the dark. Maybe they had religion.

'I'll manage,' he said.

'But have you got anything?'

'I think there may still be a handful of nuts.'

'That's not enough!'

He knew it wasn't enough. Why did she think he'd brought the rifle?'

'Perhaps – ' she glanced at her companion – 'we could slip out early tomorrow morning and bring something?'

To his relief, the black girl said, 'We can't first thing. We're on breakfast duty.'

'Oh; I'd forgotten that. Well, all right! As soon as we've finished.' She turned and addressed him, speaking slowly and with great clarity as if she thought, perhaps, he was deficient in understanding. 'We'll bring you some food and some water, and some stuff to put on your cuts. All you've got to do is just get through the night. If you really don't want to come back with us?'

'I'm used to sleeping out,' he said. 'I've got a sleeping bag.'

'Well, if you're quite sure you'll be all right – '

'I'll be all right.' He just wanted them to *go*.

They stood there, gazing at him, still seemingly undecided.

'You can't force someone,' said the black girl.

You could, of course – especially someone in the state he was. He was suddenly glad she'd thrown his rifle into the undergrowth; he began to perceive that she could just as easily have turned it on him.

They mounted their ponies at last and rode off, into the woods, with the dog, the redhead having promised that they would be back

41

'immediately after breakfast'. They would then, she said, be able to talk.

'I want to ask you questions about what it's like where you've come from – I expect you want to ask us questions, too.'

She was wrong; he didn't want to ask them anything at all. He had discovered a mad pleasure-denying sect living on the other side of the valley, which he could easily pinpoint in the street atlas if necessary. It was all the Council had requested of him. Indeed, they had specifically warned him against fraternising.

He would give them a few minutes, he decided, then start on the search for his rifle.

By unspoken consent, the two girls headed back down the hill. Scavving, now, would have seemed a very tame end to the day. They rode for a while in silence, each revolving in her mind the implications of what had occurred. It was Meta who spoke first.

'We'll have to tell Willow,' she said.

'Why?'

'You know why! It's something which concerns the whole community.'

April plaited her fingers in her pony's mane.

'Why can't we leave it till after we've talked to him?'

'What do you want to leave it for?'

'Because he's *our* discovery, and if we tell Willow she'll go and tell Rowan and then they'll want to come barging in and take over and spoil everything. And just think,' urged April, 'all the things we could find out from him and put in our papers for the exhibition!'

Meta frowned. She was never quite sure that

April fully considered the consequences of some of the actions she proposed.

'You do know,' she said, 'what he is?'

April flushed. 'A man that hasn't been done.'

'Yes. Think about it! What kind of community does he come from? No civilised people would leave men in that state.'

'You don't think he's . . . escaped from somewhere?'

April had a sudden vision of cages full of half-naked men, covered in hair, pathetically clutching at the bars. Her stomach churned. That was as bad as the olden days, people shutting up wild animals because they said they were dangerous.

'Just because he hasn't been done,' she said, 'doesn't mean he's not a human being.'

'A primitive human being.'

'Even primitive human beings have feelings.'

'Feelings?' snapped Meta. 'He was going to shoot rabbits and eat them!'

April fell silent. She had no answer to that.

'And what is he doing here, anyway? Nobody comes on a journey that long just to wander aimlessly about at the end of it.'

'Well, that's something we could ask him!' said April. 'We can make out a whole list of questions, and – '

'If Willow knew about this,' said Meta, 'she'd say for sure we shouldn't do it.'

Which was an excellent reason, thought April, for not telling her.

'What are you afraid of?' she said. 'What do you think he's going to do to us? You took his gun off him, so he can't shoot us.'

Meta pursed her lips. 'Men before they were done used to be violent and aggressive. You

43

know that as well as I do. Your history isn't *that* bad.'

'Maybe they weren't all,' pleaded April. 'Maybe only some of them.'

'Most of them,' snapped Meta. 'Why else do you think the world destroyed itself?'

'It was an accident!'

'Yes, and who caused the accident? Men!'

April gave up. There wasn't any arguing with Meta.

'Look, if we just go back tomorrow,' she said, 'with some food for him, because we promised? And then *I* promise we'll tell Willow. That would be all right, wouldn't it?'

Meta sighed. 'I suppose so,' she said.

Chapter Four

Daniel had succeeded, after the girls had left him, in locating his rifle and recovering his axe: it was as much as he had been able to do. He could barely hobble on his right ankle. His right arm was useless, and on raising his left to slash a path through the brambles and retrieve the rifle, a searing pain had gone shooting through his chest, causing him to drop the axe and double over. The pain had subsided, leaving him limp and exhausted, wet with perspiration and unable to breathe save in shallow gasps, which made any form of exertion a physical impossibility.

Defeated, he had dropped on to all fours and crawled laboriously back across the grass to his sleeping bag, his useless right arm dragging at his side. If he rested through the night he could be up with the dawn. Whether he would be fit enough to make another attempt on the Diary seemed in some doubt; but at least he could be gone from the area before the two girls reappeared.

He slept fitfully, aware all the time of throbbings in his arm and stabbings in his chest. Weird dreams or nightmares, full of meaningless violence and mad riots of colours, brilliant purples and acid greens, blood reds and bright sick yellows, all whirling in dizzying spirals in his brain, kept him in a perpetual ferment during the restless hours. His throat was dry, to the point of making swallowing a torment, his tongue like a strip of old leather in his mouth. The sleeping bag, meanwhile, had become a sodden chrysalis of sweat, sticking unpleasantly to a body over which he seemed no longer able to exercise any control.

Towards morning he fell into a sort of coma, oblivious at last of either pain or the passage of time. The first pink fingers of dawn crept unheeded over the horizon and streaked across the sky. A homegoing fox paused to investigate, unhurriedly lifting its leg and marking the spot before continuing on its way. Rabbits, unaware of their intended fate, bounded across the clearing; a few more timbers fell in the house where Frances Latimer had spent her girlhood, a hundred years ago.

The sun was high overhead, a great golden ball in the sort of sky that Frances Latimer, child of the age of pollution, had never known. Something warm and wet snaked across Daniel's burning face. His eyes slowly opened. For a second he couldn't focus, and then he saw it: the black and white dog they called Shep. It was standing over him, mouth agape in a canine grin, ears cocked forward, giving every sign of pleasure at having found him again.

Daniel struggled to sit up. As he did so, a cheerful voice called out, 'We've come! We've brought you some food.'

Daniel groaned: he had left it too late.

April rode ahead of Meta into the clearing. She wasn't sure that she was on speaking terms with Meta. Most unusually for them, they had quarrelled quite bitterly on the way there. Meta, ever cautious, had been full of her usual doubts. Suppose he had managed to get his rifle back? Suppose he was waiting for them? Suppose, even, that he had died in the night? How would April feel then? Would she still be so sure that she was right? Well, she wasn't right! They ought not to be doing this, they ought to have gone straight to Willow. A party should have been sent out. He should have been brought in, to be looked after properly.

'You mean,' had snapped April, her patience finally giving way in the face of such feebleness, 'brought in to be guarded properly!'

'Yes, I do!' had snapped back Meta. 'And why not? Until we know what he's here for – '

'He should be kept in chains?'

'He certainly shouldn't just be allowed to wander.'

'Why? What do you think he's going to do?'

'If you did a bit more reading,' had said Meta, 'you wouldn't need to ask a question like that.'

April had grown rather hot and cross.

'I know what used to happen!' It still did happen, with animals. Reading from books wasn't the only way of getting to know things. In practical terms, she probably knew more than Meta did.

Meta had said, 'Well, there you are!' as if that proved her point.

April had been silent for a few minutes, considering the matter.

'They could only have done it at certain times.'

'Well, they didn't, so that's where you're wrong! They did it whenever they felt like doing it. Even when women didn't want them to do it. It was called rape,' had said Meta, crushingly. 'They couldn't control themselves. That's why we have to remove the temptation. It's

47

dangerous, letting them go round like that. Why do you think boys are brought up separately from girls? Why do you think dogs sometimes have to be kept away from bitches? Because they're *not safe*.'

'But there are two of us,' had pointed out April, 'and only one of him – *and* he's injured.'

That, had said Meta, was the only reason she had allowed herself to be talked into this folly. And it was folly: 'You're behaving just like Harriet!'

They had bickered and squabbled all the way down the valley. It wasn't like them. They left that sort of thing, as a rule, to Holly and Linden. Part of the trouble was that April knew in her heart that Meta was right. No one had ever laid down any laws about young girls going off by themselves to talk to barbaric strangers, mainly because the community didn't believe in laying down laws but also because such a situation had never been envisaged. For all that, common sense told her that it was hardly a sensible thing to do. Perhaps she was like Harriet.

As April dismounted, she saw that the barbaric stranger, looking even more barbaric than he had yesterday, if such a thing were possible, was still lying in his sleeping bag. His eyes were open, but he made no effort to sit up. She approached him, warily. April had not had much experience of illness, for after the first few years, when the effects of the plague had still been with them, there had been remarkably little sickness in the community. Even she, however, could perceive that this was a case for urgent medical attention.

'I told you,' said Meta, coming to stand at her side. She looked down at him, critically. 'I said we should have told Willow.'

Meta *had* said it; but not for that reason.

'So what do you suggest we do now?'

The two girls turned away to confer. Daniel knew they were discussing his fate, but frankly was past caring. He wouldn't terribly have minded had they got hold of his rifle and put a bullet through his brain. He heard the black girl whisper, 'You can't!' and the redhead retort, 'He can't do anything!' They seemed to be arguing as to whether they should both ride back to base or whether the redhead should stay behind and guard him. The idea that he might be capable of doing anything of any kind whatsoever might have amused him had he not felt so utterly ghastly.

After a bit more whispering the black girl shrugged her shoulders, remounted her pony and rode off, leaving the dog and the redhead to stand guard. The dog lay down with its head on its paws, watching him. The redhead, after a moment's hesitation, squatted on her haunches beside him. He could feel her gaze upon him. With an effort, he tilted his head towards her. She was studying him, curiously, as if he were a previously unknown alien species.

'What did she think I was going to do?'

She jumped. 'I'm s-sorry?'

'I said, what did she think I was going to do?'

A betraying glow lit up her cheeks.

'If it's any comfort,' he said, 'let me assure you that I am in no fit state to do anything. If I were – ' he considered her, as she crouched by his side in the sunshine. She lacked the clear, classical beauty of her friend, but had a perky appeal of her own – 'if I were,' he said, attempting a grin, 'then it might be a different matter!'

He was delighted to see the glow flare up into a furnace, fiery red to match her hair.

'We've brought you some food,' she said. She held open the bag for him to see: bread rolls, an apple, and something that looked like dried figs. Much as he would have expected. They were obviously a sect. 'Do you want some?'

He shook his head. 'I don't think I could manage it.' He did his best to sound suitably apologetic. They had, after all, kept their word. He had been convinced they would come for him with an armed guard. Which, of course, they still might. 'The other one,' he said, 'your friend –'

'Meta. She's gone to get help. You'll be all right, we'll take care of you.' April took out a bottle of fresh water, which she had filled at the spring just before breakfast. She held it out to him. 'Would you like a drink?'

He managed to raise himself on an elbow and took the bottle from her. His hand, as he did so, knocked against hers. It was quite unintentional; he was feeling too weak to do anything intentional. But the fiery blush flew back into her cheek and she busied herself rearranging the contents of her food bag. Such bashfulness intrigued him, especially in a girl of her age. She must be at least sixteen. Surely, at the age of sixteen –

'It was lucky we found you,' said April. Meta would have hysterics if she knew he had actually touched her. The way Meta carried on you would think all pre-plague men had been like wild beasts, and of course it was perfectly true that a lot of them had been. She wasn't totally ignorant of the things that had happened in the past. But they couldn't *all* have been beastlike, or women wouldn't have tolerated it.

'Luck plays an enormous part in people's lives,' she said, 'don't you think? I think it does. I've always believed in luck – well, I'd have to, really, I suppose, being called Come Lucky April. It would be a bit odd if I didn't, really, wouldn't it?'

He could tell that she was babbling because she was nervous. He wondered what she had to be nervous of. One indisposed male, too feeble to knock the skin off a milk pudding? He, if anybody, was the one who should be nervous. He had obviously fallen in with religious cranks, and anything could happen.

'Why are you called Come Lucky April?' he said.

'Oh, well, because I was born in April, and because my mother had almost given up hope of ever getting pregnant. She'd tried and tried and it just never took. She'd decided ages ago that she'd have to give up – because otherwise it was such a waste, you know.'

Waste? he thought. Waste of what? Time, energy?

'And then on her sixtieth birthday,' said April, 'all the community got together and said why didn't she have just one more go, as a sort of birthday present, and it actually worked, and she was so happy that when I arrived she called me Come Lucky.'

There was a silence.

'Did you say . . . *sixty*?' said Daniel.

April nodded, serenely. Daniel choked, as he swallowed a gulp of water the wrong way. Either this girl was a fantasist or a lunatic. She couldn't be *that* naive. April leaned forward and took the bottle from him.

'Do people – that is, women,' he said, 'women

51

– in your community . . . do they normally have children at the age of sixty?'

'Not these days,' said April. 'They used to sometimes at the beginning, when we needed to build up the numbers and everyone wanted to do their bit. But it's not really necessary now. We're fairly stable. Of course we have to watch the gene pool but on the whole we've been very fortunate, Willow says. We haven't really had any major defects come up. Only very minor ones that we've been able to nip in the bud. Willow says it's mainly a question of keeping careful records and watching the permutations. After all, when you stop to think about it, everything had to start somewhere, didn't it? I mean, right at the beginning of time . . . there can't have been that much choice, can there? They'd just have had to make the best of what they'd got. I suppose it came down to natural selection, or something. I guess there must have been a lot of wastage.'

Daniel listened, bemused. He hadn't the faintest idea what she was talking about, and neither, he suspected, had she. It occurred to him that maybe she was a bit simple.

'What's your name,' she said, 'anyway?'

'Daniel.' He fell back again, into his sleeping bag. 'I think I've broken my arm.'

'That's all right. Willow will see to it. Do you mind me asking you questions? I don't mean to be nosy, but you're the first – ' she hesitated – 'the first *person* I've ever met from outside. I don't think there's anyone alive who's ever met anyone.' She sat back on her heels, trying to remember. Fortune was over eighty; she might have done. In the early days there had been a trickle of people, lone survivors who had

52

somehow found their way to the community. Once there had even been a band of about a dozen, all at once, but that had been in the first few months. It had been decades, now, since anyone new had turned up. 'Have you ever met any outsiders?' she said.

He grunted. 'Mm-hm.'

'So did you know we were here, or was it just chance?'

'I didn't – know you – were here.'

'So it was just chance?'

'Sort of – chance.'

'You mean – ' she was leaning forward, hands clasped between her knees – 'you mean you didn't just arrive here by accident?'

'Not – accident. I came – was looking – for something. Special. To my – family.'

'In the house?' She swivelled round to indicate it. 'In there? Is that why you went in?'

He nodded. It seemed easier, in the end, to answer her questions than to fight them off. And really, what did it matter? He would never find the Diary now. He would be lucky if he escaped with his life. He had heard tales about people who had had religion. His mother, and some of the other women who hankered after it, seemed to forget all the unspeakable things that had been done. Crucifixion, persecution, burning alive. Who knew what this particular lot might be into?

'What was it?' said April. 'This special thing? Perhaps I might be able to find it for you.'

'Too dangerous.'

'I'm an expert,' said April.

She sat, waiting for him to tell her. Haltingly, between the shallow breaths which were all that he was able to manage, he gave her a brief version of the story. Did he cherish a faint hope that she might be as good as her word? That she might indeed be able to find the Diary for him? Of course she wouldn't. And even if she did, small chance he stood of ever bearing it back in triumph as he had planned.

'That is the most incredible story,' said April. She seemed to have stopped being nervous of him. She was hunched forward, almost touching him. 'I promise you, if the Diary's there, I'll find a way of getting it for you.' She paused. 'If I do . . . would you let me show the journal to Meta?'

He frowned. Meta was the black girl.

'She's really into history. She'd go looby over it. And the Diary! They'd be the biggest things that ever happened to her.'

He was silent. The black girl was hostile to him. He had felt it coming from her, in waves. *And* she had thrown his rifle away. Why should he be expected to do her any favours?

Quickly, sensing a reluctance, April said, 'You don't have to if you don't want to. I'll get it for you anyway. That's a promise.'

Now she had made him feel churlish. He mumbled, incoherently.

'I'll come back tomorrow,' said April, 'and have a try. We were going scavving anyway.'

He wondered what scavving was. She seemed to speak a language that was the same as his and yet not.

'Your people – ' She bent her head, to hear him. 'Will they –'

'What?'

'What will they – do? Do you think?'

'To you? Nothing!' She sounded surprised; almost indignant. 'Only get you better.'

'And then – what?'

'What do you mean? Then what?'

'Will they – let me – go?'

'Why shouldn't they let you go?'

He moved his head, helplessly. It was beyond him, at the moment, to explain the complexities of his fears. She was only a girl, and an extraordinarily naive one (if not actually simple). She could not be expected to know how her leaders were likely to react to a stranger in their midst.

'You seem to have some very weird ideas,' said April. 'I don't know what it's like where you come from, and I won't ask you now because Willow is bound to do so, and besides you are not in a fit state to answer, but we are really quite civilised. After all – ' she said it with a touch of acerbity – 'we are not the ones who carry guns and shoot rabbits.'

She might have added, neither do we let our men go about like untamed savages, but perhaps that might not be quite polite, especially as he was so obviously unwell. In any case, she supposed it wasn't his fault that he was a savage. If nobody had ever told him, he possibly didn't even realise. Men had had to be shown the error of their ways; they hadn't learnt it voluntarily. There had even, initially, been some resistance, but fortunately the women, led by Dr Alison, had far outnumbered them and common sense had prevailed. It *was* common sense; it had to be. The future of the world depended on it.

'Men – ' Daniel said it with difficulty: his tongue seemed to have swelled and become too large for his mouth – 'always – eaten – meat.'

She gave him a look which would have

shrivelled the essential parts of a prize bull. It was more the sort of look he would have imagined her disdainful friend Meta giving. Maybe she wasn't quite so naive, after all.

'All the more reason,' she said.

'Reason – for what?'

For not letting them walk round in a primitive state, if that was how they behaved.

'I expect Willow will talk to you,' she said, 'when you're better.'

He wondered uneasily who this Willow was that she kept referring to. He wasn't sure he liked the sound of her.

'Willow – one of – your friends?'

'She's not the same age as me, if that's what you mean. But she lives with Rowan – that's Meta's mother – and she's one of the people I most respect. Everybody respects Willow. They respect Rowan, too,' she added, 'but Willow is more practical. She's a doctor, so she has to be. She's the one who will probably see to you.'

He felt decidedly uncomfortable at the prospect.

'You can go to sleep if you want,' said April. 'I don't expect I should be talking at you like this. I do have a tendency to talk rather a lot. It's just that it is exciting, you must admit! After all, if we are here, and you are there – ' she flapped a hand in the vague direction from which he might be supposed to have come – 'who knows how many more of us there might be in the world? I've been waiting for ages to go and explore, but somehow everybody except me seems quite content just to stay as we are. Anyway – '

His eyelids closed as she talked. She became aware, after a while, that he was no longer responding. She examined him covertly as he lay there. She was not afraid of him – at least, she didn't think she was, though of course it might be different if he were not incapacitated – and the initial feeling of revulsion was not as strong as it had been, especially now, when he was so totally at her mercy. She could take out a knife and stab him and he could do nothing to stop her.

The thought came to her out of nowhere. It sent disturbing tremors up her spine. Why even consider such an appalling act? He posed no threat – for the moment. She remembered his question, what will they do to me? and her reply, nothing! Only get you better.

She told herself that it was true. It *was* all they would do to him. They certainly wouldn't harm him; no one had ever been harmed, in the whole history of the community. Neither would they retain him against his will, which was what he seemed to fear. They might see to it that he left in a more civilised state than he arrived in, because you really *couldn't* have men walking about like savages, not if the world was going to survive. They really did need to be doctored, Meta was absolutely right, but he surely could have no objection to that? Other men didn't; why should he?

Anyway, whatever happened it would be better than being left out here to die. At least there could be no doubt about that.

Chapter Five

'You don't need me to tell you,' said Willow, 'that it was hardly a very sensible way to behave.'

April squirmed. Unlike some of the women, Willow almost never lost her temper or scolded. She reasoned even with the littlest ones. April could remember, in the past, being reduced to tears of contrition after Willow had taken the trouble to spell out the possible consequences of some particularly thoughtless piece of behaviour, whereas a sharp clip round the ear from Linnet or Fortune had left her unmoved.

Willow stood there, calmly waiting, hands thrust into the pockets of her white smock.

'We did ask him,' muttered April. 'When we first found him, we said would he like to come back with us . . . he said he'd be all right.'

'You didn't have to take him at his word!'

'No, but I – I don't think he really wanted to come back.'

'Why was that, do you suppose?'

'I think he was scared.'

'Of us?'

'Of what we might do to him.'

Willow regarded her, gravely. 'What did he think we would do to him?'

April shook her head.

'I hope you told him we were civilised?'

'I told him that.'

'And he was still scared?'

'He seemed to think we mightn't let him go. I promised him,' said April, 'that we would. That is right, isn't it?' She looked up, earnestly, into Willow's cool grey eyes. 'We wouldn't hold him against his will?

'Certainly not!' Willow spoke briskly. 'What possible reason could we have for doing so?'

'Meta says he's a danger.'

'All untamed creatures represent a potential danger. That shouldn't stop one tending their wounds or giving them shelter. One just has to bear in mind that one is dealing with an unknown quantity and remember to be on one's guard.'

'Rather than . . . taming them?' said April.

Willow paused a moment before replying.

'That would depend,' she said, lightly.

The news had leaked out and by early evening was all round the community.

'Your poor mother,' said Fortune, sternly addressing April on her way in to the refectory. 'She must be turning in her grave! The proudest day of her life, it was, giving birth to you – and this is how you repay her!'

'Now what have I done?' said April.

'Flouted all the rules of common sense and self-preservation, that's what! Not to mention courtesy towards the rest of us . . . if you discovered something that could be used for the common good, you wouldn't keep it to yourself, would you?'

'What do you think?' said April, rudely. She was sick of Fortune getting at her.

'I think you'd share it,' said Fortune, 'the same as anyone else. What I want to know is, when you come across something that's likely to be a threat to us all, why you don't think you have a duty to share that, as well?'

'Because he isn't a threat! How could he be? He didn't even know we were here. In any case, he's got a broken arm.'

'A broken arm?' said Fortune. 'Since when did a broken arm ever stop a man if he felt inclined? When I think of what some of your grandmothers went through –'

'Oh, not that again!' cried April.

'It's only thanks to them that you're able to live a life free of fear and suffering, my girl. You just be a bit more grateful and accept that some of us old ones know what we're talking about. All this glib nonsense about not being a threat! If you'd been around in the old days –'

'Well, I wasn't,' said April, 'and what are you suggesting I should have done? Just left him there to die?'

'I'm suggesting you should have had a bit more thought for the rest of the community. Bad enough to put yourself at risk, but to put all the rest of us –'

April rolled her eyes.

'Yes, and you can stop that!' said Fortune. 'It's about time you youngsters learnt a bit of respect.'

Fortune stomped off, down the refectory steps. April pulled a face. Old people needn't think they deserved respect just because they were old. She moved across to join Meta, industriously ladling food on to her plate.

'What is it this time? Oh! Delight! Green froth and yellow bile! A rare treat!'

'Shut up, it's bean casserole.'

'What's the yellow bits? Puke?'

'Yellow peppers, and I'll thank you to keep a

civil tongue in your head, miss!' John had appeared, scuttling angrily at them out of the kitchen. 'I should think you've done enough damage for one day!'

'Not you as well,' said April.

'Me as well as who?'

'You and Fortune! Couple of wittering old dildols!'

Meta said, 'April!' in shocked tones. John's face turned a waxy purple.

'Some of us round here have lived long enough to know what we're talking about. It's disgraceful. It shouldn't be allowed.'

'What shouldn't?'

'You know perfectly well,' said John. 'I don't have to spell it out. This community's survived a hundred years. We can do without that sort of thing.'

'It's all under control,' said Meta. 'Honestly! Willow knows what she's doing.'

'Does she?' said John. 'Does she? I wonder.'

'I'm sure she does,' said Meta.

'She might – but do the rest of you? All you young girls . . . what do you know? When it comes to it? Only what you've read in books. You've had no experience. Think you're so clever, some of you – ' He looked contemptuously at April, sloshing bean casserole on to her plate. 'Think you know so much better than people three times your age . . . well, don't come screaming to me, that's all I can say. Don't say you haven't been warned. I'm telling you, you're storing up trouble.'

April opened her mouth. She got as far as 'What sort of – ' before Meta's elbow jabbed her sharply in the ribs.

'You'll see,' said John. 'You mark my words, there'll be trouble.'

'Do you have to rile him?' said Meta, as they carried their trays across the room to a vacant table.

'I don't rile him. He riles me!'

'He's perfectly harmless – unlike a certain other person I could name. I notice *he* doesn't seem to rile you.'

'He hardly could,' said April, 'the state he was in.'

'I thought you said you had a conversation with him?'

'Well – yes; sort of. But I was the one who did most of the talking.'

Meta arched her eyebrows. 'How unusual! What did you talk about?'

'This and that.'

'You mean, you babbled.'

'Well, at least I found out what he's doing here! Are you going to come with me tomorrow and look for the Diary?'

'Did you ask Willow?'

'I did, as a matter of fact.'

'What did she say?'

'She just said be careful.'

'Of course, the Diary isn't really the thing that's interesting,' said Meta. 'We've got all that day-to-day stuff in books. It's the Journal I'd really like to see.'

'He might let you if we find the Diary for him.'

There was a pause. Meta pushed bean casserole thoughtfully round her plate.

'You could always just have taken it,' she said.

'Taken it?' April stared at her, accusingly. 'Without his permission?'

'Well – ' Meta shrugged. 'He wouldn't have known.'

'That's immoral,' said April.

'Not really. We'd have given it back after we'd taken a copy of it. After all, it's part of our history.'

'Yes, and it's part of his history, too!'

Meta set her jaw, stubbornly. She looked as if she might be on the verge of declaring that people who were uncivilised couldn't properly be said to have any history – something she had previously hinted at – but was prevented by the excited arrival of Holly, charging across the room with her bean casserole, followed at a slower pace by the imperturbable Linden.

'*Well!*' said Holly. She plonked her tray on to the table. 'How does it feel to be the ones responsible for letting Unbridled Aggression loose on the community?'

'Have you been talking to Fortune?' said April.

'No, to John. He assures me we are all doomed.'

'It's no laughing matter,' said Linden. 'It could raise very serious ethical questions.'

'Oh, twiddle!' said Holly. 'You and your ethical questions! What I want to know is – ' she leaned confidentially across the table – 'what does he look like?'

'Grotesque,' said Meta, 'in a word.'

'*Really?*'

'Yes, really.'

Holly turned delightedly to April. 'Do you think he looks grotesque?'

'I suppose I did a bit at first,' admitted April. 'Not so much once I'd got used to it.'

'Used to what? Exactly?'

'Do we have to?' said Linden. 'At the meal table?'

'Yes! I want to know what he looked like!'

'There are plenty of photographs in the library of pre-plague males that you can go and gawp at.'

'Photographs aren't the same,' said Holly.

'No, they're not.' Meta came unexpectedly to her support. She was more usually in agreement with Linden than with Holly. 'It's very disconcerting to see one in the flesh. I thought it was some kind of ape until it started speaking.'

Holly squeaked. 'You mean it's all hairy?'

'*He*,' said April, 'actually. And actually, he does have a name ... it's Daniel. He also, believe it or not, has a mother. *And* two sisters.'

There was a silence. Meta finished off the last of her casserole, Linden directed a long, cool look at April across the table. Holly giggled, uncertainly.

'Fancy that!' she said. 'A mother and two sisters!'

'How do you know?' Linden asked the question, gravely.

'How do you think I know? I talked to him! You can't sit in total silence for a couple of hours, can you? Not if you have any social graces at all,' said April.

Holly giggled again. 'Imagine!' she said. 'It must be like talking to someone out of the Stone Age ...'

Meta, after supper, was going to a lecture given by Rowan on 'Social Aspects of Twentieth-Century Living'. Linden said that she would go with her.

'You?' She turned to Holly.

'No, *thank* you,' said Holly.

A faint, troubled ripple crossed Linden's smooth features.

'So what will you do?'

'I'm surprised you should ask,' said Holly. Meta and April exchanged glances. Meta made the very slightest of grimaces. 'There's going to be a homecoming, if you want to know. I'm going to that.'

'Whose is it?'

'Dunno. Didn't bother to look.'

'You mean you're going to a homecoming and you don't even know who it's for?' Linden's lip curled. 'That sounds intelligent!'

Holly flushed, angrily. 'I don't want to be intelligent! I want to enjoy myself.'

'Well! Each to her own,' said Linden.

Homecomings were notoriously riotous. They were mainly male affairs, though some of the younger women and girls occasionally went along for the fun of it. They were held on the eve of a boy's return from his five years' absence from the community, and often went on half the night. The official welcoming ceremony would be performed later, but that was staid in comparison.

April and Meta had been to a homecoming last year. They had spent the evening drinking what they thought was apple juice but which had turned out to be cider, and as a consequence had woken up with raging headaches the next morning. Meta had said, never again. April had been tempted once or twice, but she wouldn't go without Meta. She and Meta didn't do things separately. They were a couple.

So were Holly and Linden; and it was plain to April, studying them both across the table, that this was some kind of crisis point. You just didn't go to a homecoming without your partner.

'Who are you going with?' said Linden, tight-lipped.

'Dell.' There was an edge of defiance to Holly's voice.

'Did she ask you or did you ask her?'

'She asked me. She knew you wouldn't be going. You never want to have a good time.' Holly scraped her chair back. 'Some of us like to try and do a bit of living before we die!'

They watched as Holly went marching across to the other side of the room, where Dell and her cronies sat giggling at one of their inane jokes.

'Dell Anna is a cretin,' said Linden.

It was true that Dell wasn't the brightest, but perhaps, thought April, she had more to offer Holly than someone like Linden. April wasn't sure that she would be able to stomach Linden for too long. She wasn't exactly the sort of person with whom you could share a silly joke or enjoy long cosy chats late into the night. It was difficult to imagine Lin and Holly ever cuddling, or even just lying with their arms round each other, as she and Meta did. Impossibly high-minded, that was Linden.

'You're coming with us,' said Meta, 'aren't you?'

'Me?' April jumped, guiltily. 'Um . . . n-no, I – um – I think I'd better stay in and finish that essay.'

'Tonight?'

'Yes, well, I mean, tomorrow we're doing something else, aren't we?' She looked pointedly at Meta. She had no intention of disclosing her plans in front of Linden. This was her thing;

66

hers and Meta's. They didn't want outsiders pushing in.

'Rowan doesn't need the essays for another week,' said Meta.

'I know, but I have to do these things while the mood is on me. If I don't finish it tonight I never will.'

Meta shrugged.

'So what are you doing tomorrow that's so important?' Linden turned her steady gaze back to April. She was Willow's cousin, and looked at times startlingly like her. 'Going out to search for more cave men?'

'That's right,' said April. 'How did you guess?'

It wasn't any use trying to think of clever retorts to make to Linden; one never could.

They left the refectory together. Meta and Linden peeled off towards the small hall, where Rowan was to give her lecture, April left the building and headed as if for the girls' house.

The community, at the beginning, had chosen the semi-rural Selsdon Hall, standing in a hundred acres of its own land, as their base. In those days the Hall, massively sprawling as it was, had been more than large enough to accommodate all their needs. Over the years, as their numbers had grown, they had spread further afield, taking over other properties in the surrounding area, until now the Hall was used purely for communal activities.

The girls' house was a large red-brick building, just outside the main gates. According to Meta, who knew about such things, it was Victorian, which meant it had been standing for over two hundred years (but even that wasn't as long as the Hall, parts of which dated back to the early seventeenth century).

As soon as she was satisfied that Meta and Linden were safely out of sight April stopped and doubled back, making for the lodge where the hospital was housed. She and Meta didn't do things separately... but this didn't really count as *doing* things, thought April. Not like going to a homecoming. This was just visiting a patient in hospital. Just being normally solicitous. And polite, to a visitor. And Meta wouldn't have wanted to come with her, anyway.

She crossed the hall and put her head round the office door. One of the senior nurses was in there, writing reports.

'Can you tell me which room the new patient is in, please,' said April.

'Sorry.' The nurse spoke without even bothering to look up from her writing. 'Not allowed visitors.'

April's face grew hot and flushed. 'But I was the one who found him!'

'Can't help that! Those are my orders.'

'But I need to speak to him! I have to ask him something.'

The nurse raised her head. She looked at April, irritably. It was Heather, one of the older women. Older women tended not to approve of April.

'I've already told you, he is not allowed visitors.'

'Who says he's not? Why isn't he?'

'That,' said Heather, 'is no concern of yours.'

April was on the point of protesting, yet again, that she was the one who had found him, when a door opened and Willow appeared.

'April,' she said, 'what seems to be the problem?'

'I want to ask Daniel something. About tomorrow. I couldn't remember –' it wasn't true: she could remember everything – 'I can't remember what he said, exactly.'

'I'm afraid I can't let you disturb him just at present, April. I know you feel a personal interest, and that is understandable. However, you must appreciate –' she placed an arm about April's shoulders, gently escorting her to the door – 'that it is not that easy. We have to – think about things. We have to – make decisions. Ask me again tomorrow, when I've had the chance to sleep on it. All right?'

It was what she had secretly feared, that they would spirit him away and keep him as a semi-prisoner. Disgruntled, she walked back out through the gates and down the lane. Holly and Dell and one or two of the others were coming towards her. They must be on their way to the homecoming, they were all decked out in their finery, Holly in a shiny white body suit all hung about with beads, Dell in multi-coloured leggings and a black top. April had tried on a pair of those leggings once, but Meta hadn't liked them.

'Genuine twentieth-century man-made fibre,' pleaded April. 'All the rage once.'

Meta still hadn't liked them.

'Have those two gone off to their draggy lecture?' said Holly.

'Come with us,' said Dell. 'Come and have a good time, for once.'

April hesitated. She and Meta didn't do things separately . . . but the lecture *was* draggy and it was too late to go in now, it would already have started, and she really didn't fancy staying at home all evening by herself.

'All right,' she said. 'I'll just look in and say hello. Have you discovered who it's for yet?'

Dell giggled. 'Does it matter?'

No; she supposed it didn't, really. Only to the people concerned. And maybe to the other men in the community. She supposed they must have the same sense of comradeship as the women had.

'You don't think in a way it's a bit like...' She couldn't think of the word she wanted. 'Gatecrashing,' she said. 'You don't think it's a bit like gatecrashing, going to one of their things?'

'It's supposed to be for everybody,' said Holly. 'Not just them.'

'Yes, I know, but do you think they really want us there?'

Dell giggled again, except that this time it was more of a snigger.

'I should think after five years deprived of the sight of us they'd be only too happy!'

The others neighed their appreciation. But why should they want to see *us*, thought April, any more than we want to see them? Dell and the others were only going so that they could get a bit drunk on cider and scream and make a noise and feel that they were living. They didn't care whose homecoming it was.

She wondered, as she tacked on behind, what it was like being a boy and being sent away for five years. Did they mind being sent away? Or did they look forward to it? It seemed to April like a sort of exile. But they went away as barbarians and came back civilised and that was how it had to be. She knew that; you couldn't let men like Daniel loose on the community. But that was no reason for Willow refusing to let her see him! There had to be some way she could get in. Perhaps if she managed to find the Diary . . .

Rowan, she knew, would be wild to see both the Diary and the Journal, but the Journal in particular. The Diary might come in useful as a bargaining tool. Here is your Diary, please may we look at the Journal? Naturally she would point out to Rowan and Willow that as she was the one who had found it, she was the one who should be allowed to present him with it. She was pretty sure Rowan would agree; it was Willow she would have to convince. But until she actually managed to lay her hands on it –

'Wake up, dozy!' Holly nudged her sharply in the ribs. They had reached the house where the homecoming was being held. It was a house that was occupied mainly by the younger men – the same house where April had been last year with Meta. She was not going to repeat her mistakes: this year she would make very sure what it was she was drinking.

Dell pushed open the door and led the way confidently through the hall and out into the garden at the back. A group of boys greeted her boisterously. Dell was obviously a familiar figure at homecomings. Within seconds, she and Holly and the others had gone giggling off across the grass, leaving April by herself. April could have gone with them, there was no reason why she shouldn't, but already she was wondering why she had come. Where was the fun in being at a party on your own? She ought not to be here; she and Meta didn't do things separately. It was different, Meta going to a lecture with Linden. You didn't go to lectures to have a good time, you went to learn things. In any case, out of the corner of her eye she had just caught sight of Delian. That decided her. Where Delian was, so John was likely to be. Only let him see April without Meta and he'd do his best to make trouble for her the next day, from the sheer love of being spiteful.

'Going to parties on our own, now, are we? I told you you were asking for it, bringing that creature into the community.'

He'd take the greatest delight in linking it to Daniel. He'd been wittering on all day like the voice of doom. Him and Fortune, with their heads together. 'Your poor mother, after all she went through . . .'

April turned, to go back into the house. As she stepped through the door, momentarily blinded by the comparative darkness of the interior after the early evening sunlight outside, a low voice said, 'Hallo, April!'

She jumped. 'Who's that?'

A figure stepped forward. 'Don't you recognise me?'

'D-David?'

'Have I changed that much?'

'N-no, I just – hadn't realised – you startled me, that's all!'

She laughed, trying not to sound as awkward as she felt. Years ago, as children, David Tessa and April had played together. David had had friends amongst the boys, and April even then had had Meta, but there had been a special bond between the two of them which had led them, quite often, to pair off and invent their own games away from the others.

April remembered, with sudden vividness, playing stepping stones across the river. She remembered the tree house they had built, and the den they had made in the bracken. The tree house, for all she knew, might still be there. The little kids might be playing in it even now as she and David had done.

'So how are you?' said David.

'I'm fine,' said April. 'How are you?'

'I'm all right.'

He was a year older than April. He had gone away with the other boys when his time had come and she had missed him for a while but soon forgotten, as children will. She couldn't recall when she had last thought of him; maybe not since he had gone away.

'You're looking good,' said David.

'So are you,' said April. It was an automatic response; politeness decreed that one could not say otherwise. But there was something about him which troubled her. The David she remembered was a sturdy, blond-haired, blue-eyed twelve-year-old, not quite as boisterous as some of the other boys but more than willing to follow wherever she chose to lead – usually somewhere Meta had refused to go, which usually meant trouble. It was with David she had set out on an expedition up the river and very nearly drowned: with David she had cooked potatoes in the den and set fire to the bracken and tumbled out of the tree house and got lost down in the valley. She found it hard to believe, looking at him now, that this was the same boy. He was taller, of course, and older, just as she was, and with the same blond hair and the same blue eyes. But there was an air of gravity about him, almost a bleakness, which was disturbing, even to the not particularly observant April. Meta could be solemn, but she didn't go round as if she had the weight of the world on her shoulders.

'Is this – ' she waved a hand, indicating the merriment taking place in the garden – 'is this for you?'

'You came without knowing?' he said.

'Well, I – yes. I mean, it's not something I usually . . . it was Holly's idea. I just came at the last minute.'

'I see.'

He had thought she was there specially, because the homecoming was for him. April blushed, hotly.

'If I'd realised, I'd have brought Meta.'

If she'd bothered to think, she would have known David was due back.

'Is it just you, or – '

'Me and a few others.'

He named them, but the names meant nothing to her. Doubtless they had been around when she and David had played together, but David was the only one who had ever held her attention.

'When did you get back?'

'This morning.'

'This *morning*? Why haven't I seen you?'

The community wasn't so large, even now, that you didn't bump into everyone sooner or later as you went about your daily business.

'I saw you,' said David. 'Several times.'

'So why didn't you come and speak to me?'

'You were always so busy – doing things. With other people.'

'You could have come and interrupted!'

'I wasn't sure that you would want me to. There seems . . . such a gulf. I never noticed it before. It struck me almost the minute I got back. Have things changed, or was it always like this?'

'I think it was always like this,' said April. It seemed to her quite natural. You grew up, you grew apart, there simply wasn't that much communication between younger members of the sexes. How should there be? They lived their own lives, pursued their own interests. Age might bring them into closer contact, but during the years of their maturing they had little enough in common. Even at homecomings girls tended to dance together, whilst boys gathered in groups to talk and drink.

'After all,' said April, 'we're not children any more.'

'No; I suppose that's it.'

'Well, it has to be, doesn't it?'

'Does it?' said David.

'Well – ' She shifted, uneasily. What did he want from her? What did he expect? Once they had been children and had played together: now they were older and must go their separate ways. It was the same for everybody. She had never known anyone question it before.

'Don't you find it rather sad?' said David. He obviously did.

'I suppose it is, a bit. But it's just the way things are.'

'And you like the way things are?'

She had never really thought about it. The way things were was the way things were. How else could they be?

'You don't feel,' said David, 'that we might have . . . got it wrong?'

She wrinkled her forehead. 'Wrong how?'

'The way we . . . arrange things.'

'But they've always been this way,' said April.

'Not always,' he said.

She looked at him, uncomfortably. What was he trying to say? He surely wasn't suggesting they revert to barbarism? Involuntarily, her thoughts switched to Daniel, kept behind locked doors in his hospital bed. The only way, she thought, was to find that Diary. It was the only chance she had of being allowed in.

'I'm obviously upsetting you,' said David. 'You'll have to forgive me. I'd forgotten what it was like, back in the community.'

'Did you want to come back? Were you looking forward to it?'

'Yes.' His mouth curved in what was almost a parody of a smile. 'I was, as a matter of fact.'

'It hasn't disappointed you, has it?'

'Don't journeys always end in disappointment? *"To travel hopefully is a better thing than to arrive, and the true success is to labour".*'

'Pardon?' April blinked. 'What's that?'

'Something I once read somewhere . . . we do read, you know. Some of us.'

She was indignant. 'Did anyone ever say you didn't?'

'Not in so many words. But I've hardly been back twelve hours and already I'm beginning to feel a bit like a performing animal . . . like a dog walking on its hind legs. *"It is not done well; but you are surprised to find it done at all."'*

'I'm sure you read a great deal better than people like Holly,' said April. And then, quickly changing the subject: 'Where have you been assigned? Or haven't they decided yet?'

'Yes, I'm working with Willow.'

'Willow?' Her eyes widened in genuine astonishment. Very few people, not even

women, were selected to work with Willow. It was what Linden was hoping for. 'That's incredible!'

'Yes, I can see you might find it hard to believe . . . I get the distinct feeling that not very much is really expected of us.'

'That's not true! That's simply not true! It's a pity you weren't here last month, we had a debate on that very subject . . . why weren't there more men in positions of responsibility in the community.'

'And why weren't there? What was the conclusion?'

'Well, partly that the percentage of men to women is obviously a lot smaller to begin with –'

'That, I suppose, being taken for granted.'

'Yes. Well – I mean . . .' Why waste resources? Men simply weren't as useful as women. You didn't need as many. In the old days they'd had no choice, but when you did have a choice you obviously chose what was going to be of most benefit to the community. Even David must see that.

'All right.' He nodded. 'So what were the other reasons?'

'Partly that you spent so much time away from us – we actually discussed that,' said April. 'We discussed whether to bring you back earlier – but mainly that you don't tend to push yourselves forward enough.'

David's mouth twisted again in that parody of a smile. 'You want it both ways, don't you?'

'Want what both ways?' said April. She waited, but he only shook his head and didn't answer. 'It's not that *we* don't think you're capable of taking responsibilty, it's you that don't seem to think you are. Anyway, it was agreed that you've got to be encouraged. Maybe that's why you've been chosen to work with Willow.'

She could see at once that it was the wrong thing to have said. His face darkened. He said, 'Thank you for that vote of confidence. And there I was thinking I'd been chosen purely on merit.'

'Oh! Well, but I'm sure you have. I didn't mean – it's just – well, Linden, for example, will *fight* to get where she wants, but all too often you'll just take a back seat.'

'Like I said,' said David, 'you want it both ways.'

She looked at him, doubtfully.

'Anyway,' he said, 'that's enough of me. How about you? What are your plans?'

'None, specially.' She would just be an ordinary average member of the community, turning her hand to whatever was needed. 'I'm not gifted like Meta or Linden. Or you,' she added, hastily. One shouldn't put men down just because they were men. There were some who had made really outstanding contributions to the community. They were just so ... *creepy*. She didn't like to be around them. David was different. He was David, and there was a special bond between them; and anyway, he was still young. For the first time it struck her, as being rather sad: would David grow up to be like John and Delian?

'From what I've been hearing,' he said, 'it sounds as if you're destined to lead expeditions into the unknown ... you were always good at that, weren't you? Do you remember the time we got lost in the valley and they had to send out a search party?'

'Yes, but I don't get lost any more.'

'No, you go out and find other people who are lost . . . what is he like, this – person – you brought back?'

'I didn't bring him back, Willow did, and some of the others.'

'But you found him.'

'Me and Meta.'

'So what is he like? Is he . . . like us?'

'Different,' said April.

'Different how?'

It was difficult to say different how. 'Haven't they let you in to see him?'

'Me?' said David. 'You really think they'd let me anywhere near him?'

'Why not?'

'Me or any of us?'

'I can see why they won't let any of *us*. I can't see why they won't let you.'

He looked at her, long and hard. 'Try using your imagination,' he said, 'if you've got any.'

April watched, in bewilderment, as David turned and strode out through the double doors into the garden. Now what had she said to upset him? She didn't remember him being touchy like this. April had always been the one starting the quarrels, picking the fights – not that she had ever picked a fight with David. What had happened to him, to make him so bitter? Well, she knew one thing that had happened to him, of course, but that happened to all the boys, it was a normal part of growing up. She didn't see why that should make him bitter. Everyone had to grow up.

She stood frowning, staring out into the garden, watching as David joined a group of young men being toasted by some of their elders. Now that she saw them, she was able to link them up with the names he had given her . . . Harry Alexandra, Simon Fay, Martin Gail. They didn't look bitter. They were laughing and fooling around, cracking jokes as young men did. David, in spite of having joined them, didn't really seem part of them. He accepted a drink that was put into his hand and she heard him laughing, but she could tell, even from where she stood, that it was a forced laugh, assumed for the occason, for the sake of being sociable. There was something very sad about it.

It distressed her to think of David being sad at a time when he was supposed to be celebrating his re-entry into the community. Traditionally, homecoming was a big occasion for young men. There would be an official welcome by the whole community, but it was the unofficial get-together, organised by the men themselves, which really counted.

She was reluctant to leave on a sour note. She knew a moment's impulse to go after him but the sight of John and Delian coming across the lawn towards her changed one impluse to another and took her hastily slipping back out into the hall and through the front door. She didn't want John poking his nose in, and besides, what comfort could she offer David when even now she was not sure what it was that troubled him?

She put David from her mind. David would still be here this time next month: Daniel might not. Concentrate, Meta always said, on one thing at a time; get your priorities right. Her priority at this moment was to find the Diary. It was, she was convinced, her sole chance of ever getting to see Daniel – ever getting to hear about that outside world she so craved to explore. Now they had positive proof that another community existed, there would surely be some move to mount an expedition, to establish whether there might be more? If there were to be an expedition, then April wanted to be part of it. She wanted it more than she had ever wanted anything. Even if it meant coming back afterwards and settling down to a normal humdrum community existence, at least she would have been there – at least she would have *seen*. The Diary was the key to it. Find the Diary and they could hardly deny her the right to present it to Daniel in person.

She would have an early night, she decided. Scavving could be tiring, and this was one time when she was determined not to fail.

Chapter Six

'It's no use,' said Meta. She stood, looking in through the doorway of no. 10 Raglan Court. The dust had settled again and a pile of rubble filled the hall. The stairs had disappeared, buried beneath it; the top landing sagged, still shedding the occasional chunk of plaster. 'We're wasting our time. There's no way we're ever going to get up there.'

'There's always a way,' said April. 'It's just a question of finding it.'

'We need a proper search party, with equipment.'

'No, we don't!' April didn't want a search party. She wanted to find the Diary by herself.

'You're not going inside?'

'Of course I'm not going inside!' What did Meta think she was? Brain-damaged, or something? In any case, there wasn't any point in going inside; that wasn't the way to tackle it. She was surprised that Daniel should have made such an elementary mistake. Did they not have experience of scavving, where he came from?

'The Diary was in the cupboard by the side of her bed . . . beds were upstairs, right?'

'Not necessarily,' said Meta. She only said it because she was feeling argumentative.

'Well, if you think it's going to be *down*stairs that would make it even easier!'

What did she mean, even easier? 'You mean,

it would make it marginally less impossible. Actually,' said Meta, 'in a house like this she probably would have slept upstairs. And there is just no way – '

'Trees?' said April.

The only tree growing within anything like striking distance of the upstairs front window was a holly bush. Sturdy enough to climb, no doubt – but who would want to?

'You'd get scratched to pieces,' said Meta. 'And I'm not sure the top branches would take your weight.'

'I bet they would, but maybe we ought to try round the back first. Don't you think she's more likely to have slept at the back?'

'Why?'

'Because she was the child. They always slept at the back.'

Meta wrestled with the concept. There was nothing in her reading which would lead her to suppose such a thing. What was the logic of it?

'Whenever we've found children's stuff,' said April, 'it's always been at the back. Usually. Except sometimes when it's been in one of those little rooms over the vehicle places.'

'Garages,' said Meta. 'This one's got a little room.' She could just make out the window, hidden behind a thick mass of creeper.

'Yes, but if she was the *only* child – '

'How do you know she was the only child?'

'I said *if*. If she'd had a brother or sister she'd hardly have gone off without them, would she?'

'She would if they were dead. Most people did die,' said Meta.

'Oh, all right! Let's say she had six brothers and eight sisters and they all got the plague and they all died and she slept in a hole in the *ground*. I am still,' said April, 'going to try round the back before I try at the front!'

Meta watched in glum silence as April marched determinedly to where they had tethered the ponies and began unstrapping one of the saddle bags.

'Why do you always have to do everything in such a mad rush?' she said, as April came back with the saddle bag and the two scav poles.

'I'm not doing everything in a mad rush.'

'Yes, you are! It would have been far more sensible to wait till we could organise a proper party.'

'That might have taken weeks. Daniel will be gone by then.'

'So? We're not doing it just for him, are we?' Because if so she certainly wasn't risking her neck for some barbarian savage that went round carrying guns.

'Look,' said April, 'if we find the Diary he'll let us read the Journal. He might even let us make a copy of it. And then it could go into the Archives . . . "discovered by April Harriet and Meta Pauline." That would be something, wouldn't it?'

'You don't have to treat me like a child,' said Meta.

'Well, but where is your spirit of adventure? You're supposed to be a historian – you're supposed to be *interested* in the past! I'm only a humble artisan.'

'Oh, shut up,' said Meta. 'Give me those shears.'

Daniel had woken in what he assumed to be the early hours of the following morning – the sky through the window was still flushed with the first pink streaks of dawn – to find himself in a bed, with some kind of cover pulled over him. He had turned his head on the pillow, trying to work out where he was. His impression was that he was in a room on his own, at any rate he could see no other beds or hear any other sound of breathing, but even the mental effort involved in sitting up, never mind the physical one, was beyond him. He was simply too lacking in energy. He had registered only the fact that he seemed mercifully free of pain before his eyes had closed and he had sunk back into unconsciousness.

He was roused some time later by a light touch on the shoulder. His eyelids sprang open, body tensed with immediate suspicion. Was this it? The moment of truth? A voice – man's or woman's, he couldn't make out – spoke from somewhere above him.

'Relax. No one's going to harm you.'

If it didn't sound exactly friendly, at least it didn't sound overtly threatening. He raised his head the necessary couple of inches and saw a man – woman? – in a white smock standing over him.

'How are you feeling?'

'Better – I think.'

'You've been suffering from concussion. You have a lump on the back of your head the size of a pigeon's egg.'

'Oh.' He put up his left hand, experimentally probing.

'You've also broken your arm and cracked a couple of ribs. And done something to your ankle.' The voice, indeterminate as ever, droned out his injuries like a litany. 'We think it's a bad sprain rather than a break. You won't be able to walk on it for a while.'

He received the news in silence. The prospect appalled him. It would have appalled him in any circumstances, but to be incarcerated hundreds of miles from home, at the mercy of some mad pleasure-denying sect who for all he knew could turn out to be sun worshippers or –

'Do you want to sit up?'

It was more in the nature of a command than a solicitous inquiry. The creature, whichever sex it was, had already hooked an arm round him and was busy hauling him up the bed. He winced and gritted his teeth, though the pain was not as bad as it had been.

'I've brought you some food.'

A tray was placed before him. On it were a pitcher of milk, a plate of bread and butter and a dish containing what looked like mashed eggs. He realised, as his attendant picked up a spoon and placed it in his left hand for him, that he was actually quite hungry. He realised also, what he hadn't realised before, that the lower part of his right arm was encased in a plaster splint and that his body was swathed in some kind of garment, tentlike and all-engulfing, but fastened only at the neck like a cape, so that it gaped open as he sat.

The attendant said, 'I'll leave you to get on with it. If there's anything you need, just ring the bell.'

Daniel nodded. Under the smock he could see trousers, made from a coarse, dark blue material. The creature had, presumably, to be male, though even now he found it hard to tell. It could just as well have been a middle-aged female. Its face was soft and jowled, without any sign of either beard or moustache. Its body shape, in the smock, was too ill-defined to give any clue, and the voice, equally, was of no help.

Boldly, Daniel said, 'I'd thank you if I had a name to call you by.'

'Common hospitality needs no thanks.'

'Well, but I'll thank you anyway,' said Daniel. 'Common courtesy demands no less.'

There was a pause. Daniel dug awkwardly with his spoon into the mashed egg.

'My name is Daniel,' he said.

'Delian.' The information was given with obvious and tight-lipped reluctance, as if the handing over of one's name to a total stranger was the surrender of something precious to which he had not earned the right. And even now he was none the wiser. Delian? He had never heard the name before.

He finished his breakfast, messily, using his left hand. The androgynous Delian returned and removed the tray, came back again with a bowl of water and cloth, sponged him down – not roughly, but nonetheless with marked distaste – told him to stay where he was and rest and that 'Willow would be here to talk to you shortly.'

The door closed, leaving Daniel to his own devices. He looked about the room. It was small and cell-like, with latched window and whitewashed walls, two of which he could touch by simply stretching out a hand, and no furniture save a chair, a cupboard, and the bed on which he lay. He pondered again the question of Delian's maleness or femaleness. From the distaste so plainly expressed he had to come down, despite the trousers, in favour of the latter. A fearsome breed of women, if so. He wondered uneasily whether the all-powerful

Willow would be in the same mould.

After a bit, defying the order to stay put, he worked his way to the end of the bed and rather shakily wobbled to his feet – or foot – to look out of the window. By supporting himself with one hand against the wall he was just able to maintain a precarious balance.

There was little enough to be seen. He could make out a gravel path, and trees, but no one came by and in the end, growing bored, he switched his attention to the door. If he sat on the extreme edge of the bed and leaned forward he could just reach the handle. Carefully he tried turning it: the handle moved but the door did not. Evidently they had locked it. It was not reassuring.

He eased himself back against the pillows. Almost immediately, he heard the sound of a key being turned. The door opened and a head looked round. Again, he couldn't for the life of him have said whether it was man or woman. It was younger than Delian, beardless and prettyish, a bit on the plump side. A pair of round brown eyes gazed at him across the room.

'Did you want something?'

'No, I was just taking a stroll round the estate,' said Daniel.

He grinned, to show that it was intended as a joke rather than sarcasm. The eyes flickered down to his bare feet and up his body to his face. There, for a moment, they rested. A shadow of something which looked uncommonly like repulsion passed across the bland features. No answering grin met Daniel's.

'It would be better if you stayed in bed. Willow will come when she can.'

'It's all right, it's all right!' Daniel threw up

his left arm in a gesture of conciliation. 'I'm not complaining!'

The door closed; he heard the key turn again in the lock. He looked round for his pack and found it in the cupboard. Upon inspection, it seemed to be complete and as he had left it. The copy of Frances Latimer's Journal was still there, buried under the several layers of clothes which his mother, ever anxious, had pressed upon him. He took it out and began to read.

I am at present residing, if that is the right word, in a second-hand bookshop halfway along the Edgware Road, in London. With me is Shahid Khan, who is a boy I was at school with.

Shahid Khan; his great-grandfather. It was as much as he knew about him. No indication in the Journal as to where he lived or what he was like, though at one point there was a complaint that he was becoming 'masterful'. His family, it seemed, had had religion. Frances wrote how 'Shahid explained how his brother was a devout Muslim and looked upon Shahid as an infidel.' Other than that –

He turned his head sharply as he heard again the sound of the key being turned. He was just in time to catch the door opening, the merest crack, before promptly closing again.

A mistake? Or were they spying on him?

He went back to the Journal.

For a short time my best friend Harriet Somers was with us, but Harry left to go to the party. This was a party which was being held in Trafalgar Square, and which I expect was well over by the time she got there.

Harriet had disappeared, never to be heard of again.

I have to accept that something has probably happened to her. I am trying not to think about it. There are lots of things I am trying not to think about; this is just one of them.

She had returned to the subject of Harriet several times in the Journal.

Sometimes I think that Harry was actually far braver than I am, because after all it's surely better to go out with a bang than just hang on, which is what I am doing.

And then, towards the end:

The twelfth day. It has happened" a rat has got in. I opened the door into the shop and there it was, on the counter. I screamed soloudly that it took off, but Shahid

He froze, as the door opened yet again. Another of the strange androgynous faces peered furtively round. Another pair of eyes stared at him.

'Were you looking for something?' said Daniel.

'Sorry. Got the wrong room.'

The door closed, the key turned. Slightly unnerved, Daniel returned to his Journal.

– Shahid says that is it, we are not staying here a minute longer. I am just going to write a note to Harry before we leave. I am going to tell her where she can find us and pin it to the door, just in case.

He lay back, the Journal resting on his chest,

wondering, as Clem had so often wondered, if they had ever managed to discover what had happened to the wayward Harriet. Had she had an accident, as her friend Frances plainly feared? Had she been raped, murdered, died of the plague? Or had she after all been a survivor? None of the records showed that she had ever turned up in Cornwall, though admittedly the records from those early times were sketchy. People had been too busy getting themselves sorted out to bother over much about posterity.

Twice more as he lay there, waiting for the promised arrival of the unknown Willow, the key turned in the lock, the door was edged open and curious faces peered at him. On each occasion the faces were smooth and beardless, yet he was almost sure, by now, that they were men. Not a hundred per cent sure; but almost. He was beginning to feel decidedly queasy.

It was a relief when at last the key turned, the door was flung open and someone who was unmistakably a woman walked in. She was wearing one of the white smocks over a pair of dark blue trousers, but this time he could be in no doubt. He knew it had to be Willow even before she introduced herself. He remembered the little redhead, April, telling him that Willow was 'one of the people I most respect'. Looking at her, he thought that Patty would respect her, too. There weren't many people whom Patty respected.

'Hallo! I'm Willow.' She held out a hand. She was the first person not to recoil from him. Even the redhead had had qualms until she had grown used to him. Truth to tell, he was beginning to have a few qualms of his own.

'Delian tells me you're feeling better.'

'Much better, thank you.'

'Good!' With an air of brisk authority she pulled the chair up to the bed and sat down. Daniel, suddenly prurient, drew the cover over himself. He felt embarrassed, clad as he was in his tentlike shroud.

'Now,' said Willow, 'we have to talk.'

He nodded. Yes; talk. They had to talk. He had questions to put, things he needed to know, things –

'Is that all right?' said Willow.

'Of course.' He shook himself. She was only a woman, for all her cool air of authority. An attractive one at that, in spite of being, as he would guess, in her mid-forties. She had kept her shape well; not bagged like most of them did. She certainly wasn't pretty, her face was too strong for that. He supposed she would be called handsome. It was a pity she had her hair pulled back. It was thick and springy, the colour of ripe chestnuts. It would have softened the angles of her face, made her more feminine, if she had worn it loose. But still she was a good-looking woman. Daniel could relate to good-looking women – certainly better than he could relate to the weird unsexed dolly creatures he had seen earlier.

'I have a request to make.'

'Oh?' He stiffened, instantly wary.

'It's nothing so very terrible, but it would be greatly appreciated if you would remove your –' she hesitated – 'your beard,' she said.

The relief was such that he almost laughed. What had he thought she might be going to say? He didn't know, save that the frequent appearance of the plump smooth faces round the door had started to make him feel decidedly jumpy.

'I take it that gives you no problem?'

It gave him none at all, save as a matter of principle. He toyed with the idea of digging his heels in, thought better of it and said, 'Am I at least allowed to ask why?'

'To go clean-shaven is the custom of our people. Facial hair is found to be disturbing.'

He raised an eyebrow. 'Has anyone complained?'

'Not in so many words, but you know how it is.' She spoke apologetically. 'At different times in history, different customs prevail . . . there was once a time when the sight of a woman's ankle was considered positively indecent!'

'I suppose that wouldn't account for my strange succession of visitors, by any chance?'

'What strange succession of visitors?' Her tone was sharp. 'Who has been in here?'

'A person by the name of Delian?'

'Delian has been assigned to you. He is your personal carer.'

'Oh! So he's a he, is he? I couldn't decide whether he was a man or a woman.'

She ignored that. 'The others?'

'I couldn't decide whether they were men or women, either.'

She frowned. 'I gave strict instructions you were not to be disturbed! They have absolutely no right to come bothering you.'

'They didn't bother me, exactly. They just shoved their heads round the door and ogled.'

'You have to appreciate that you are the first person we've seen from the outside for more than a generation. You're naturally an object of some curiosity. Nonetheless, that is no excuse for bad manners. I beg your pardon; I'll see that it does not occur again.'

'That's all right. I don't want to get anyone into trouble. I don't mind being stared at – just so long as I know what it is that's doing the staring.'

'I dare say we are objects of curiosity to you just as you are to us. However, we can explore our differences at some other time.'

He would have preferred to explore them right now and either set his fears at rest or at least allow them to be confronted head on; one or the other. It was the not knowing which caused prickles to run down his spine. There was definitely something about this community which worried him. Before he could wrap his tongue round the question which was forming in his mind, the woman had smoothly moved the conversation into safer channels.

'I gather from April you came here in search of a diary which belonged to your great-grandmother. That is extremely interesting! She and Meta have gone off this morning to see if they can find it for you. If they can't, we might consider sending out an official search party.'

He muttered, 'That's good of you.'

'Oh, don't run away with the idea that we'd be doing it purely for your benefit! Such a document would have great historical value for our community, as well as personal value for you. I'm working on the selfish assumption that if we find it you would have no objection to our making a copy? Also – ' her eyes slid to the Journal, lying on the bed beside him – 'I believe you have a record of her journey from here down to Cornwall at the time of the plague?'

His hand closed protectively over the pages

which Clem had so painstakingly transcribed for him. 'Only the first twenty-two days. Up to the point where she left London.'

'It must make fascinating reading. I shan't press you now, but I have to warn you that our historian is almost certainly going to lay siege to you at some time or another! I don't know whether April told you, but we are setting up a special centenary exhibition to celebrate the founding of the community ... a copy of the Journal, if you would allow us to make one, would be a prize exhibit!'

He chose not to respond to that: two could play at being evasive. He said, 'She didn't mention anything about an exhibition. But she did tell me how she got her name.'

'April? Yes, we've tended on the whole to choose names that have some significance for the months in which we're born ... you'd never believe it, but I was actually called Pussy Willow! All very well when one is a child, but not really suitable for a grown woman, I can't help feeling.'

He refused to be sidetracked. Stubbornly he said, 'She was telling me about her mother.'

'Scilla? Yes, she was a most courageous woman. A great personality. She died, unfortunately, last year. A tremendous loss to the community.'

'But she must have been – quite old?' He performed some speedy mental arithmetic. 'At least ... seventy-six?'

'About that. But we are a long-lived bunch. It is not at all unusual to survive into one's nineties.'

'And to bear children in one's sixties?'

He half expected her to laugh, and tell him

that April had been adopted and simply having a bit of fun at his expense. Instead, very seriously, she said, 'I suppose that must strike you as strange?'

'Where I come from,' said Daniel, bluntly, 'it would strike me as impossible.'

'Yes; I can see that where you come from it most probably would.'

His hackles rose at that. Who the hell did she think she was to use that patronising tone towards him?

'Being brought up in the sort of society you obviously have been, you are probably not aware,' said Willow, 'that technically it is perfectly possible for an older woman to be implanted and carry a child to term. The technique was available even before the plague, though it was not in common use. But in the first decade of our existence it helped us overcome several of the problems we were faced with. Since then, as our needs have changed, it has become largely redundant.'

Just as well, he thought. Playing around with nature! It was disgusting. What kind of people were these? Rode about on horseback eating vegetables, yet had the technique to mess with people's innards? No wonder they made him feel queasy.

'May I ask a question?' he said.

'By all means! Ask whatever you wish; we have no secrets. What is it you want to know?'

'In theory . . . am I free to go?'

'You are free to leave whenever you choose. The only thing which could detain you is the extent of your injuries.'

'And the key in the door.'

'The door has been kept locked for your own

protection. I have already apologised for the intrusions. It will certainly not occur again.' Willow stood up. 'I shall leave you now. Try to get some sleep. I'll come back when you're feeling stronger and we'll continue the discussion. In the meantime –'

In the meantime, he was at their mercy; and still knew very little more about the set-up than he had five minutes ago.

'I do assure you,' said Willow, 'you are perfectly safe.'

He only wished he could believe her.

'It's all *right*,' said April. 'Don't fuss! I'm perfectly safe.'

She didn't look safe. She had crawled out along the branch of a sycamore, which had grown up close to the back wall of the house and thrust its way through one of the windows. Meta, waiting below, expected any moment to hear a scream and find April plummeting earthwards.

'Safe as houses!' called April.

But houses weren't safe. Houses collapsed. Houses rotted. Houses –

'Pass me a scav pole!'

With mute obedience, Meta pushed one up. There was a busy rustling amongst the branches, then April's voice again: 'And the other!' The second scav pole followed the first.

'What's happening?'

'I think it's the right room. I can see a bed . . . and a cupboard – what's left of it. It's in a hideous state. The room, I mean. There's green gunge all down the walls and some of the floorboards have fallen through.'

'Whatever you do, don't go in!'

'I'm not going to go in. I can reach from where I am.'

Meta heard a series of bangs and scrapes, which was presumably April manipulating her scav poles, interspersed with ominous creakings from the branch she straddled with so much confidence. A chunk of rotten timber came crashing to the ground, followed by a shower of bricks. Meta had visions of the entire wall collapsing; it had happened before now.

'This is *easy*!' cried April. 'The door's come off!'

'What door?'

'Door of the cupboard.'

'Is there anything in there?'

'Yes, I'm just – trying – to . . . got it!'

'Got it?'

'Nearly. It'll be all right,' panted April, flailing about her with her scav poles, 'so long as the floor doesn't – give way.'

'Why?' Meta peered apprehensively up through the branches of the sycamore. 'You're not in there, are you?'

'No, I'm trying to – drag it – over here –

'Is it the Diary?'

'Not sure. It's all – wrapped up in – oops! *Ouch*! Damn! *Ow*! Blast! I've dagged myself. Hell!'

April sat back on her branch, sucking vigorously at the side of her hand. Meta shook her head. She thought, I will never come scavving with April again. She was too old for scavving, anyhow. It was a kids' game.

'Catch this!' yelled April.

Something came slithering through the branches. Meta made a snatch at it and missed. While she was scrabbling after it in the undergrowth, a triumphant April appeared at her side.

'Told you we'd find a way, didn't I? Where is it? Let's have a look!'

'Watch it!' said Meta. 'It might be fragile.'

'All right. You do it.'

Carefully, Meta picked off the remains of what had been the outer wrapping. It was brittle, almost like glass, but in places had adhered to the surface of the book inside. She could just faintly make out some lettering: Marks & S –

'Look!' Meta was enchanted. 'Marks & Spencer!'

Marks & Spencer had been one of the big repositories of the twentieth century, where people had gone to purchase things with the notes and coins which they had been given in exchange for their labour. Many of the clothes in the community store had come from Marks & Spencer.

'Marks & Spencer!' marvelled Meta. 'She must have gone there . . . this must have been one of their bags. She must have put it in there to keep it safe.'

She imagined some far-off girl at the end of the doomed century tenderly wrapping her most treasured possession in the hope that it would outlive her and one day, in the distant future, be discovered.

'She must really have wanted someone to come along and find it.'

'So now someone has,' said April. There was no room in April's heart for sentimental imaginings. Very much a person of the moment was April. 'Stop maundering over it and check whether it's the right thing.'

'Well, it's a book,' said Meta. 'Do you want me to open it?'

'Just a tiny bit, to make sure it's hers.'

Meta eased back the cover, half expecting it to come away in her hand, but the Marks & Spencer bag had done its work well: the book looked to be in the same condition as it would have been when it had last seen the light of day, a hundred years ago.

Eagerly, April peered over Meta's shoulder. There, on the inside cover, in neat printing, they read: *Frances Latimer, 10 Raglan Court, South Croydon, Surrey. HER DIARY*.

'That's it!' April made a lunge and grabbed at it. Meta winced: April had *no* feeling for history. 'We mustn't read it before I've shown it to Daniel. It's his, not ours.'

He won't appreciate it, thought Meta, sourly. (She didn't care for the familiar way April referred to him by his name, as if they were friends. In her own mind, if she referred to him at all, she referred to him as *him*.)

'I think we deserve to have a look at it.' She pushed her hair back, defiantly. 'Considering we're the ones who found it.'

'But it's his,' said April. 'He came all this way for it. Just because he's – like he is, doesn't give us the right to cheat him. He can't help being like that. It isn't his fault.'

'That's the excuse they always made . . . *they* couldn't help it: it wasn't *their* fault.'

'Well, they couldn't,' said April. 'And it wasn't.' She picked up the scav poles and tucked them under her arm. 'They weren't civilised then like we are now.'

In any case, she didn't want to share the Diary with Meta, she wanted to share it with

Daniel. Meta could see it afterwards. April had found it, April was going to give it to him; and then he would tell her all those things that she was so desperate to know. The outside world . . . not as it used to be; a hundred years ago, you could read about that in books. What it was like *now*.

She hugged the Diary jealously to her.

'Let's hurry up and get back!'

Chapter Seven

'I thought,' said April, 'that as I was the one who found it —'

'You ought to be the one to give it to him.' Willow nodded. 'I don't dispute the justice of that. But what about Meta? Didn't she help?'

Not really, thought April. I could just as well have done it by myself.

'It would seem fairer if you both gave it to him.'

'I don't think Meta particularly wants to.'

'Nevertheless,' said Willow, 'I would prefer that you went together. You're not a child, April. I don't want to have to exercise control over you, but I do expect you to behave sensibly. Ask Meta to go with you, and I shall have no objection.'

'You've got to come with me.' April announced it glumly to Meta, as they met up later in the kitchen. They were on lunch duty for the next few days, an assignment April specially loathed as it meant working under the supervision of John. He always took the opportunity to give her all the really foul tasks, such as washing fifty kilos of potatoes or chopping vast piles of onions, which made her eyes stream.

'I told her,' said April, 'that you didn't want to, but she insisted.'

'What did you expect? She'd let you in there alone with him?'

'Why not?'

'Don't be naive!'

'Well, it's ludicrous! There are at least a dozen people within earshot. I'd be perfectly safe.'

'That's what they all used to say,' said Meta, darkly. *'I'll be perfectly safe* . . . and then they ended up raped and murdered and dumped in ditches with their throats cut.'

'Oh, for goodness' sake!' April had no patience with such talk. She was sure it was all exaggeration. Of course there had to be *some* truth in it, she accepted that; but all the same . . . 'I'd only have to scream!'

'Yes, and by then it might be too late.'

'Precisely.' John came across, humping a vast sack of freshly dug turnips. 'Get this lot scrubbed and stop being vainglorious. You've no more idea than a babe in arms. We've successfully wiped out all that sort of thing. We don't want it back again, thank you very much – and no more you'd like it if we did!'

April, tipping water into the sink, said: 'How can you talk like that when you haven't even seen him?'

'I don't need to see him.'

'Aren't you even tempted?'

'No, I am not,' said John.

'Not even to have just a tiny weeny peek?' Even Holly had been interested to know what he looked like.

John pursed his lips.

'You mean, you have no intellectual curiosity at all?' said April.

'I'll tell you what, young woman.' John pointed at her with his long, sharp kitchen knife. 'If I had my way I'd use this on him . . . that's as far as my intellectual curiosity extends.'

'Pathetic!' said April; but she was shaken, nonetheless. It was the first time she had ever heard anyone express the wish to use violence towards another living creature. People argued, of course, and sometimes swore, and the little ones quite often fought, but that was as far as it went. There had been real venom for a moment in John's voice.

'What did you expect?' said Meta, as they stood at the sink together endlessly scraping the earth off five thousand turnips. 'You can hardly blame him.'

'Why not?' April said it truculently. It was going to take them all morning, scrubbing this lot. She knew he gave her and Meta the rottenest jobs on purpose.

'Because, basically,' said Meta, 'he represents a threat.'

'Who? Daniel?'

'Obviously.'

'A threat to him?' April jerked her thumb contemptuously over her shoulder.

'To all of them.'

She must have looked blank, for impatiently Meta said, 'Use your imagination!'

It was what David had said: *use your imagination – if you've got any.*

'You mean, in case he turns violent?'

'No, dummy! I mean that being a barbarian he still has all those – ' Meta glanced over her shoulder and lowered her voice, out of consideration for John – 'all those primitive urges that they don't have any more.'

'So? How's that supposed to make him a threat?'

'Oh, for goodness' sake!' Meta sounded exasperated, as she sometimes did when April failed to follow her train of thought. 'It's basic psychology. He's got something they haven't. It might make them feel . . . well! Inferior, or something.'

'But they're *civilised*.'

'Yes, and so long as everyone else is civilised there's no problem. You get some barbarian marching in, and – '

'And what?'

'Look,' said Meta, 'you've either got a brain or you haven't. If you have, then you don't need me to spell things out to you. If you haven't, there's no point in talking to you. Why don't you just give the Diary to Rowan and let her deal with it?'

'Because I'm the one who found it and I don't see why I should. And anyway, I'm more likely to be able to talk him into letting us see the Journal.'

Meta's eyes narrowed, suspiciously. 'How do you work that out?'

'Because I was the one who stayed with him. He trusts me.'

'You don't think,' said Meta, viciously slashing the top off a turnip, 'that you're developing an unhealthy fascination for him, do you? It's like in that old play we read where someone falls in love with an ass.'

April flushed. 'Who said anything about falling in love?' That was sick! 'I'm interested, that's all.'

'Well, I'll come with you this once,' said Meta, 'but I'm *not coming again*.'

It wasn't very successful, going to see Daniel with Meta. She had known it wouldn't be. How could you hold a normal friendly conversation with someone while all the time a third party was sitting glowering on a chair, exuding hostility at every pore? It naturally made Daniel hostile, too, so that what had begun in quite promising fashion, with him thanking them for the Diary, and sounding really pleased and happy about it, and April solicitously inquiring after his various injuries, speedily degenerated into a prickly disputation between him and Meta.

There were a thousand and one questions that April would have liked to ask, and she scarcely had the chance to ask a single one. Meta launched into her attack almost straight away, deliberately goading him, inquiring with serpentine sweetness whether the food was to his liking and hoping that 'you are not missing the taste of dead flesh?'

Daniel had removed all the hair from his face. He didn't look nearly so outlandish without it, especially sitting up in bed in a hospital gown, so that you couldn't see the hair on his body. You could almost forget that he wasn't the same as other men.

He parried Meta's first thrust quite amiably, obviously not wishing for confrontation any more than April.

'Meat,' he said, 'is what we call it.'

'You can call it what you like,' said Meta. 'It's still the flesh of murdered animals.'

'If you're so keen on not murdering them — ' he said it mildly enough, though looking pointedly at Meta's leather skirt — 'how come you have no objection to wearing their skins?'

'Animals do die of natural causes, you know,' said Meta. 'Or maybe, on second thoughts,' she added, 'where you come from they don't.'

Quickly, April said, 'We see nothing wrong in making use of animals after they're dead. It's

106

just that we would never kill them.'

'So if you make use of their skin, why not of their flesh?'

She recoiled. 'We're not carnivores! We feed the carcasses to animals who are.'

'Is food so plentiful,' he wondered, 'that you can afford to waste it?'

'We do not regard it as waste,' said Meta, haughtily, 'if it helps other creatures gain nourishment.'

'At the expense of human beings?'

Meta raised a frosty eyebrow. 'We all have equal rights to life.'

'Not in my community,' said Daniel. 'In my community it's people who have rights. We care first and foremost about human beings.'

'That is one of the differences between us,' said Meta. 'Here, we care for all forms of life. We think there has been quite enough killing.'

It was at this point that the first faint flicker of irritation appeared in his eyes.

'Are you religious?' he said.

Meta drew herself up. 'Certainly not! We are an advanced civilisation.'

'Advanced?' He looked round him, at the bare room. 'I don't see any signs of technology!'

'*Socially* advanced. That is where we have concentrated our energies.'

'Do you have technology?' said April, eager to slip in one of her questions.

'No.' He shook his head, almost impatiently. 'Not any more. We don't have the resources. But then – ' he swung back to Meta – 'we don't call ourselves an advanced civilisation!'

'You hardly could,' she retorted, 'going round with guns, shooting living creatures! That's not very civilised, is it?'

Stung, he said, 'I didn't carry guns only to shoot wild life. I carried them for self-defence.'

'Self-defence?' Meta's eyebrow shot back up. 'Against what?'

'Against whatever might be out there. You're not telling me you'd set off into the unknown without some sort of protection?'

'If by protection you mean *guns* – ' said Meta, at the same time as April said, 'We never set off into the unknown.'

They stopped.

'Well, we don't,' said April.

'But if we did,' said Meta, 'we certainly shouldn't carry guns.'

'We couldn't,' explained April. 'We haven't got any.'

'You must have had some originally. They were all over the place.'

'I daresay,' said Meta.

'It was a question of priorities,' said April. 'Food and shelter seemed more important than weapons.'

'They still do,' said Meta.

'You'd change your ideas fast enough if someone attacked you!'

There was a silence. They sat there, contemplating him.

'Who would attack us?' said Meta, at last.

'There isn't anyone,' said April.

'There's me, isn't there?' He challenged them. 'What would you have done if I'd pulled a gun on you?'

Meta shrugged.

'Why would you have done that?' said April.

'And how would it have made things any better,' said Meta, 'if I had had a gun as well as you?'

108

'Well, since I was wounded and you weren't, you'd probably have managed to get in first. Self-preservation,' said Daniel, 'is what it's all about.'

'You mean, I would be alive and you would be dead?'

'Whereas this way,' said April, brightly, 'you're both alive. That's got to be better.'

Meta and Daniel both ignored her.

'Just because nobody ever *has* attacked you,' said Daniel, 'doesn't mean nobody ever will. Who knows what might not be out there?'

'Now that we've met you,' agreed Meta, 'it does rather make one wonder.'

April stepped in again, quickly. 'You see,' she said, 'we had no idea there were still any primitive communities in existence.'

Daniel stared, first at her and then at Meta. 'Who's she calling primitive?' he said.

'It's not intended as an insult,' said Meta. 'It's simply a way of describing levels of civilisation . . . the late twentieth century was technologically advanced but socially quite primitive, we are technologically primitive but socially advanced, you appear to be both technologically *and* socially primitive.'

It obviously riled him. 'Considering you know next to nothing about us,' he snapped, 'I'd be extremely interested to know how you arrive at that conclusion! Do you condemn a community as primitive solely on the grounds that they continue to eat meat? As, I would remind you, men have done for thousands of years.'

'*Men*,' said April.

'And women! Don't kid yourself!'

'Eating flesh is certainly primitive,' said Meta, 'but of course it's only one part of the whole.'

'The whole being – what? Exactly?'

The two girls exchanged glances.

'I don't think Willow would want us to discuss it with you,' said Meta, suddenly become prim. 'You had better take it up with her.'

'Don't worry,' he said, 'I will!'

'Yes. I thought that sooner or later you would want to know,' said Willow.

'Is it unreasonable? I'm stuck here, in a locked room –'

'I told you before, you are free to leave at any moment you choose. You have only to ask.'

'And how far would I get? In this state?' He indicated his right arm, still encased in its plaster cast. His ribs remained sore, and breathing painful, his ankle too swollen for him to do more than hobble to the commode (which with eyes averted one of the strange dolly men – or were they women? He still hadn't been able to decide – emptied for him twice a day. Not a word was ever exchanged. Perhaps they were under orders not to fraternise with the enemy).

Bitterly, he said, 'You're offering me a freedom I can't afford to take.'

'Give it a couple of weeks and you should be mobile.'

'And what do I do for those couple of weeks? Sit here waiting for the key to turn in the lock and heaven knows what to come bursting in?'

'I've given you my word,' said Willow. 'No one will come bursting in.'

'Look, forgive me – ' he tried not to sound patronising, even though she was a woman. He sensed that in this topsy-turvy place it would not go down too well. 'How do I know,' he said, 'that your word is any good? And even if it is . . .

110

how do I know you're in a position to enforce it?'

'You don't, of course – and I'm not. Nobody is. We don't organise ourselves on that basis.'

'So your guarantee is worthless!'

'No; I'm just being honest with you. I can advise people, and I believe they will listen to me. But it's true there is no absolute guarantee. I realise I'm asking you to take rather a great deal on trust.'

'Which I might be a bit more willing to do if I knew what the plague was going on!'

'What exactly is it that you want to know?'

'Well, for one thing – ' he said it bluntly. To hell with her sensibilities – 'why have they sent you here to talk to me rather than one of your leaders?'

'I think I had better sit down,' said Willow. 'I can see that we are going to have a rather long talk.'

She seated herself on the chair, next to the bed. She was carrying a sheaf of papers and looked brisk and businesslike. He found it disconcerting: it was not what he was used to.

'First of all, let me correct you on one point: no one *sent* me. I came of my own volition, as a representative of the community. Secondly, we do not recognise leaders in any official sense of the term. Not one of us has any absolute authority vested in her. Does that answer your question?'

Far from answering it, it only raised a dozen more.

'Where I come from – ' He stopped, wary of inviting mockery.

'No, go on,' she said. 'Where you come from – ?'

Stiffly he said: 'It would be more usual for a man to do the talking.'

111

'Ah! Yes. I see. So that's what's bothering you.'

'I find it curious, that's all. I've been here for over forty-eight hours and I still haven't seen one.'

'Haven't seen one?' She looked at him, reprovingly. 'How can you say so?'

'If you're referring to Delian, then all right, I'm sorry, I apologise, one ought not to mock the afflicted, but when I said I couldn't decide whether he was male or female I was telling no more than the truth. I didn't intend any insult.'

'Nevertheless, he would take it as such.'

'Well, I've been pretty insulted by him, if you want to know! In my community,' said Daniel, 'people acting as carers don't openly show their disgust to the patients they're supposed to be looking after. Maybe that's because all our nurses are women, not eunuchs. They might not be able to produce babies at the age of sixty, but at least they know better than to make you feel you're something that's just crawled out of a cesspit!'

He noted with satisfaction that the flawless ivory of Willow's face had become very faintly tinged with pink.

'I beg your pardon,' she said. 'I was afraid something like that might happen. I'm sure he doesn't mean it, but – ' She stopped. 'I'll get one of the older women to be responsible for you.'

'It doesn't have to be an older one,' he said. 'What's the matter? You think I can't be trusted? You think I'm going to jump up with a broken arm and ravage someone?'

Willow compressed her lips. She obviously did not find it amusing.

112

'What exactly was it,' she said, 'that you wanted to know?'

'Men,' said Daniel.

'That's right. You asked why you hadn't seen any, apart from Delian. But you have seen some. The – how was it you referred to them? Your strange succession of visitors?'

'You call those *men*?'

She corrected him, coldly. 'We don't *call* them men: they are men.'

He stared at her, revolted; not willing, even now, to believe what her words would seem to imply.

'I did warn you,' said Willow, 'that our philosophies are very different. However – ' she crossed one leg over the other, clasping her papers to her chest – 'to set your mind at rest, and because we are a totally open society – we have no secrets; why should we? – let me tell you something of our history.'

He wanted to say, 'The hell with history! Just tell me what's going on,' but there was something about this woman that stopped him. She wasn't openly hostile, as Meta was, but he sensed a cool certainty, almost a superiority, in her attitude which at one and the same time incensed him and made him anxious not to appear the uncivilised boor they all so obviously thought him.

'We started off,' said Willow, 'as a small group of survivors – as no doubt you also started. It just so happened that the women in the group outnumbered the men by about three to one. Of those women, several were beyond child-bearing age, but obviously one of our priorities, as a group, other than day-to-day survival – which presented relatively few difficulties,

113

given the amount of foodstocks available at that period – was viability in terms of numbers. In other words, we needed to breed.

'So, as I already explained, we made use of what was then quite innovative technology. The reason we were able to do this was that one of our number was a doctor, a woman who had specialised in that particular field. In that, we were lucky. We were also lucky that she happened to be a woman of strong views and strong personality. If it hadn't been for her, and some of the other women who supported her, we might well have ended up as I suspect you have ended up: a primitive – ' *again*! He bristled, but kept quiet – 'a primitive patriarchal community dominated by men.'

'Instead of which – ?'

'Instead of which we are a civilised matriarchal community dominated by women.'

He was tempted to ask how that was supposed to be any better, but there were more pressing questions waiting to be answered.

'So how did you arrive at this . . . civilised state?'

She smiled fleetingly, acknowledging the unspoken quotes round the word civilised.

'Not without a struggle! It was decided in principle, from the start, that we would organise ourselves democratically – and I do mean democratically. Not the pseudo-democracy of the twentieth century. We wanted none of the old ways of government. Everyone was to be free to have a say – and an equal say. This worked reasonably well for the first few years, but then as some of the young boys started to mature the older men began to grow more confident and flex their muscles, and gradually, bit by bit, the old ways began to creep back in – '

'When you say the old ways?'

'Men asserting themselves at the expense of women. Men taking over the running of things, making the decisions – '

He refrained from pointing out that this was only natural. Instead, he said, 'If the men were so outnumbered, it has to be assumed that the women allowed it to happen?'

'Yes, it was the old story: we were unwilling to compete in the face of male aggression. It was not our way of working. We prefer co-operation. Compromise. Discussion. We also had different objectives. The men wanted us to put all our efforts into maintaining what technology we could. One of the things they wanted was to amass an arsenal of weapons, purely, of course – ' a note of sarcasm crept into her voice – 'for defensive purposes. A familiar pattern – doubtless repeated in your society. In the end, needless to say, the inevitable happened. A small group of men gained control and pronounced themselves leaders. It would not surprise me to learn,' said Willow, 'that in your society there is still a small group of men who style themselves leaders.'

He said nothing to this, refusing, for the moment, to be drawn. He had more personal matters at stake. Willow waited, smiled, and continued.

'It was at this point that Dr Alison came to the fore. She called a meeting of all the women and put it to them: did they want a society run on the old lines, or did they feel the time had come for a change? Did they, in other words, want a society organised by women for the benefit of the community as a whole or a society ordered by men for the benefit of men?'

Daniel opened his mouth and immediately closed it again.

'You wanted to say something,' said Willow.

He waved a hand. 'Carry on.'

'The women decided, unanimously, that the time had come for a change. They didn't feel they had survived the nightmare of global catastrophe only to go on in the same old way, with men leading them to yet more disaster. It was then put to them, did society really benefit from the presence of men at all? In short, did society really *need* men? Or had they outgrown their usefulness?

'I have to tell you,' said Willow, 'that by a very large majority, almost 100 per cent, it was decided that they had. After that, the way was clear. We had the means, we had the expertise, thanks to Dr Alison. Artificial insemination had been practised for centuries. Our advantage over our ancestors was that we now had the means not only of — collection, but also of storing. We use solar energy, of course, and a certain amount of wind power. We had only to convince the men of the wisdom of what we were proposing — '

'Never tell me they went along with it!'

'Surprisingly, one or two of the older ones did. It was the younger ones who were not quite so enamoured of the idea.'

'Would you have been?' said Daniel. 'If you were a man?'

For a moment the mask slipped: the same naked hostility that manifested in Meta showed itself.

'Would you be so enamoured of being raped, of being murdered, of being brutally beaten, if you were a woman? Would you be so happy to have been caught up in wars that were none of your making? To have watched your world being polluted and torn apart and finally led to disaster?'

'You can't possibly say that was all the fault of men,' he protested.

'Who ran the world? Not women!'

'So if they were content to sit back passively and let it happen –'

'Maybe it was in their natures to be passive just as it was in men's natures to be aggressive.'

'Not all men!'

'As a generality.'

'So if women sat there and did nothing, weren't they equally to blame?'

'Perhaps so – or perhaps no one was to blame, given our human nature. But there was a problem which needed to be coped with, and the women of our community coped with it in the only way which presented itself. Those men who stood out were given the opportunity to leave if they wished – a few did. Most stayed. Those who stayed were not touched in any way at all; we only demanded that they did nothing to interfere with the democratic decision which the community had taken. From that point on we have lived in peace. We still have the need of a few male babies, of course, but we are able to regulate our numbers.'

'And by the time they're – what? Fourteen? Fifteen?'

'Fifteen,' said Willow, 'as a rule. Twelve is when we send them to the boys' house –'

'And fifteen is when you –' He couldn't bring himself to say it.

'Castrate them.' Willow said it for him, quite pleasantly.

117

'And that is what you call *civilised*?' It almost took one's breath away. The sheer effrontery of it. 'You accuse me of being primitive while you're – treating people like animals!'

'Yes.' She nodded, quite calmly. 'And why not? We treat our animals extremely well. We neuter our male cats and dogs to prevent them from overpopulating. That is perfectly true. As human beings we don't at the moment have any problems in that direction. In fact – ' she gave a small, frost-nipped smile – 'thanks to the folly of your forebears I should say that that is something humanity will not be faced with again for at least another few thousand years. But problems of aggression and dominance . . . they were still with us. They had to be dealt with. And we have dealt with them. You'll find very little of either in this community.'

'That may be so. That may very well be so. But at *what price*?'

'You think it is a high price? Well, perhaps it is – but the price of doing nothing was even higher. That was a price we were not prepared to pay. In the meantime, let me assure you that our male babies are cherished every bit as much as the girls. We make no distinction of importance between one sex or the other. Every man or woman has an equal right to have her say in the running of the community. We are all free to speak our minds, to express our opinions without let or hindrance. No one has ever sought to prevent men holding positions of responsibility on the grounds that their sex disqualifies them.'

They scarcely could, thought Daniel, considering they no longer had any sex. He felt, for a moment, quite sick.

'There is only one flaw,' he said, 'in your perfect society.'

'What is that? – I never claimed it was perfect, by the way.'

'You say everyone has an equal right to have their say, but if the men – ' the word almost stuck in his throat as he said it – 'if the men are in such a minority how can they ever hope to change things?'

'That is assuming they would wish to change things.'

'Yes, well, let's assume just that!' said Daniel. 'Let's assume for a start they'd like a chance to grow up as nature intended.'

'The question has been raised from time to time as a debating issue. It has always been heavily defeated – largely by the men themselves. I think if you were to ask them you would find them perfectly content with the way things are. You must appreciate that things have been this way for very nearly a hundred years. It seems to them quite natural.'

'But it's not, and you know it!'

Willow shrugged. 'Human beings stopped living in a state of nature as soon as they evolved into human beings. We've always tinkered and tampered. So now we've reached a stage where men in their natural state are . . . superfluous to requirements. It may seem harsh, put so bluntly, but that is how it is. Without them, for perhaps the first time in history, we are able to live in harmony.'

His lip curled.

'You never fall out? You never have disputes?'

'Oh, to be sure! We may be women, but we are only human. Human beings are far too complex to get along without rubbing one another up the wrong way. But we are not armed and we have no power factions; no one need live in fear of violence. Not even – ' Willow stood up, clasping her papers to her chest – 'a primitive male who wanders in from the outside. I thank you for removing your beard, by the way. Psychologically it makes it easier for our people to – cope with you. And I believe,' said Willow, with a rare touch of humour, 'at any rate from what I have read, that they do grow again fairly quickly?'

'*If* nothing is done to prevent them,' said Daniel.

'I have given you my word. We don't seek to impose our ways upon others, so long as they don't seek to impose theirs upon us.'

'I'm not really in a position to do much imposing, am I?'

'In that case,' said Willow, 'you have nothing to fear.'

He looked at her. 'No?'

'What must I do to convince you? Would it set your mind at rest, I wonder, if I were to send one of our men to talk to you?'

One of the weird unsexed dolly creatures? '*Delian*? No, thank you!'

Willow shook her head.

'Not Delian; Delian is of a different generation. I can perfectly understand that you and he would have little to say to each other. But one of the younger ones . . . David, perhaps. I have a feeling that you and David might get on rather well. I'm sure he'd be only too happy to answer any questions you cared to put to him.'

'Having been carefully primed beforehand, no doubt.'

'Oh, dear!' Willow sighed. 'You are an

extraordinarily cynical young person, aren't you?'

'Not normally,' he said.

'Well, let me assure you that David is one of our brightest stars. He has no need of being primed, he is perfectly capable of answering for himself. You are obviously not accustomed to hold intelligent conversations with women. Possibly you'll find it easier to discuss your fears with another man.'

Bestowing upon him one of her sweetly condescending smiles, Willow had left the room before he had a chance to make the obvious retort. If this David had been subjected to the same iniquitous treatment as all the rest then he had forfeited any right to be regarded as a man. What kind of *man* would meekly allow it to happen? He was damned if they were going to get him that easily! Crippled he might be, but he didn't intend going down without a fight.

His eyes roved the bare cell in search of a possible weapon . . . nothing! They had removed the razor they had brought him with his early-morning washing water, likewise all his lunchtime cutlery.

He opened the door of the cupboard. The shelf inside was removable: he removed it. It wasn't much, but it was better than nothing. And he wouldn't hesitate to use it on that smug bitch, either. He had never hit a woman in his life, but there were some women who asked for it. Willow was one.

Chapter Eight

'I understand you wanted to see me?'

The door had opened and a boy had come in. He stood there, stiffly, on the edge of the worn rug which was the only form of floor covering. He was about the same age as Daniel, roughly the same height but of slighter build. Blond-haired, blue-eyed — fair complexion, regular features. Patty, no doubt, would find him attractive. A bit too clean and well-scrubbed for Daniel's taste, but at least, thank God, there was no question which sex he was. Or had been. He thought, once again, what kind of man would voluntarily submit himself to the hands of these screaming viragos.

He said abruptly, 'Are you David?'

'Yes. Willow said you wanted to ask me some questions.'

'*I* didn't say I wanted to ask you any questions. That was her idea, not mine.'

The faintest of faint smiles crossed David's face. 'That's Willow for you.'

'You mean she manipulates people?'

'Let's just say she has a certain way with her.'

Daniel laughed; shortly and without amusement. 'You can just say that. Personally, I'd put it rather more strongly.'

'She's been giving you a rough time?'

'Frightening the living daylights out of me, if you want to know the truth.'

David frowned slightly. He hadn't bothered to

draw up the chair but stood leaning with his back against the door, gravely regarding Daniel.

'I wouldn't have thought she was a particularly frightening person.'

'No, well, that's probably because you're used to her. You're accustomed to have women boss you around. I'm not.'

The blond head tilted, proudly.

'I don't let anyone boss me around, man or woman. Besides, we don't operate that way.'

There was a pause.

'An unfortunate choice of word,' murmured Daniel, 'in the circumstances. Are you telling me they didn't boss you around when you were however old it was . . . fifteen? Isn't that what she said? When you were fifteen years old –'

A small spot of colour appeared in David's cheek, but his gaze remained steady.

'Most of us tend to put our faith in adults when we're that age.'

'A pity in your case it was so misguided.'

The small spot of colour changed from pink to crimson.

'On so short an acquaintance you really feel you're entitled to express an opinion?'

'Bloody right I feel I'm entitled to express an opinion! What's going on here is a crime against humanity! What the hell do these women think they're playing at? Trying to rewrite history? Make it into her-story?'

'They could hardly make it any worse than it was before.'

'You stand there – ' you, deprived of your manhood – 'and calmly say that? They mutilate you and then you defend them?'

The flush deepened. 'It's not a question of

defending. It's a question of understanding the historical perspective.'

'Balls to the historical perspective! There's no historical perspective that can excuse this sort of thing!'

Curtly, David said, 'I don't believe I used the word excuse.'

'Look, sod the intellectual nitpicking!' Anger had overtaken him, the raw, blazing anger that he had held in check with Willow. It swamped all reasoned form of argument. 'What you've let them do to you is an outrage! And I'm here to tell you that if anyone tries it on with me –'

'No one will try it on with you.'

'They bloody well better hadn't! Because no way would I go meekly to the chopping block. Maybe you couldn't help it, you were just a kid. But you'd think to God –'

'What would I think to God?'

'You'd think to God that when you were old enough to come to your senses some of you would speak out! But of course she wouldn't have sent you here if there was any danger of that, would she? You're obviously one of her trusties.'

The shaft hit home. For the first time an answering spark of anger blazed in the blue eyes.

'I'm nobody's mouthpiece, if that's what you're implying.'

'No, you've just been brainwashed and aren't even aware of it!'

David breathed, deeply. 'I can't attempt to answer that. Maybe this will answer it for me.' He held out some pages, neatly clipped together. 'Here.'

'What is it?'

'Something I wrote. I thought it might – explain things a bit.'

Daniel glanced at the top page. It was headed, "Croydon Community Centenary Paper: David Tessa." Swiftly he ran his eye down the first few paragraphs. He looked across at David, puzzled, and with a new respect.

'Do they know you've written this?'

'Probably, by now. They didn't last night, when Willow asked me to come and see you. I handed it in this morning. I – '

David broke off as someone on the other side of the door turned the handle. He stepped forward into the room. The door opened and a tall, bronze-skinned woman walked in.

'Ah, David,' she said. 'Willow thought I might find you here.' She advanced upon the bed, one hand held out. 'Good morning! I'm Rowan – Meta's mother. I thought I'd just look in and introduce myself. How are you?'

'All right,' he said. 'Thank you.'

'Good!' She smiled at him. She seemed, on the surface, nowhere near as formidable either as Willow or as her own daughter. He might almost have been deceived into thinking her sympathetic – prepared to overlook the fact that he was a primitive male whose unchained aggressive instincts might cause him to jump on her at any minute. He quickly became aware, however, that beneath the amiable façade there was a layer of unrelenting steel.

'I thought,' she said, 'that you might like to see some of the essays that our young people have written for our centenary exhibition.'

She held out a sheaf of papers. He glanced swiftly at David and then away again. He was still holding David's essay in his left hand, where the woman could scarcely fail to notice it. She made no comment, however – possibly on the principle that once the horse had bolted there was not very much to be gained from closing the stable door – merely placed the fresh bundle on top of his bedside cupboard.

'If you would care to write one of your own, as a visitor to the community, it would be most interesting for us to have an outside view.'

'You're taking rather a lot for granted, aren't you?' he said. 'You really think I'm capable of putting pen to paper?'

It gave him a malicious satisfaction to see a dark circle of red appear on her cheeks. Her skin wasn't as dark as her daughter's: she couldn't hide the fact that he had succeeded in embarrassing her. He stole another glance at David, but David stood there, impassive.

'Relax,' said Daniel. 'I was only joking. But it is rather an advanced accomplishment for a primitive male, don't you think?'

Recovering, she said, 'We have never underestimated men's mental abilities. I'll leave these papers with you. Maybe when you've read them we'll talk again. I'm sure we should both find it instructive – David, Willow said she's sorry to drag you away but she could do with a bit of a hand in the dispensary, if that's all right.'

'Of course.'

Of course, of course. Of course it was! Of course she could! Discovered her mistake, hadn't she? Thought he was to be trusted, didn't realise he had a mind of his own. At least they hadn't managed to destroy him completely, although upon reflection he wasn't so sure that that didn't make the crime even more heinous.

Someone like Delian would probably never have amounted to much anyway; but this boy —

The door closed, he heard the key turn in the lock. He glanced again at David's essay, then, out of curiosity, picked up Rowan's sheaf of papers. The words 'It was men that caused all the trouble' leapt at him from the top page. Angrily, he flipped through the others. All written by girls, as you would imagine. Rosemary, Linden, Holly, Hazel . . .

He came to one that said 'April Harriet'. It struck him that none of them seemed to have proper surnames: April Harriet, Holly Fay, Linden Alison. Alison had been the name of the women who was responsible for it all. He wouldn't be surprised if somewhere they had a statue of her. He pulled out April's paper and cast an eye down the first page.

'. . . order of society reversed . . . men who were the dominant sex . . . aggressive and liked fighting . . . still be aggressive today if it were not for their training.'

Training! So that was what they called it. He tossed April's paper contemptuously to one side. Weren't there any written by men? So-called men.

He found only two. Both so cringed with crawling apology for the sins of their fathers — 'the disaster was man-made. Men were to blame for all the evils of the world' — that it was all he could do not to crumple them into a ball and hurl them across the room. Brainwashed lackeys!

He turned back again to David's.

It was true that up until at least the end of the twentieth century it was men who wielded most of the power. This is undeniable. What cannot be readily ascertained is why this should have been so. Was it, as some have maintained, that from the dawn of history might was right and the physically stronger sex gained ascendancy over the weaker? Or was it, as others have claimed, that women's horizons were narrower than men's, thus by their very nature keeping them within the more limited confines of home and family?

Daniel nodded. It seemed to him self-evident. Girls like Patty were the exception; and even Patty would moderate as she grew older.

The question was rendered academic by the outbreak of plague which devastated the world. How men had gained power became secondary to the consideration of what they had dome with that power – i.e. wipe out virtually the world's entire population, both human and animal.

Those few who were left re-grouped and women took what then appeared the only course open to them to prevent a repetition at some future date of the catastrophe which had occurred. By limiting the number of men in society and by physically removing the cause of their aggression they have proved that human beings are in fact capable of living in harmony with one another.

Whether there are other post-plague communities which have taken the same drastic if seemingly logical step is not at present known, though it would be interesting, should contact ever be established, to discover whether alternative methods of controlling the male of the species have been found or whether, without such control, the old male hierarchy still holds sway and the old order continues.

It was the only sane note he had heard. He wished they could have talked for longer, though short of telling the poor guy what he was missing –

A sudden scraping sound, coming from the window, made him look up. A face was peering at him. Another of the lackeys, eager for the sight of a real man?

He swung his legs down from the bed and eased himself upright. He still had to watch how he moved or the stabbing pain in his chest was liable to take his breath away, but at least now he was able to set his foot on the ground without too much agony. Another couple of weeks, Willow had said. He put it at ten days at the most. (It would, he thought, be as much as he could take if he didn't want to crawl home a nervous wreck. Of all the horror stories he had been regaled with before he had left, no one had ever come up with anything quite as horrific as this.)

It was the redhead, April, bobbing about outside the window. She pointed imperiously at the latch; obediently he lifted it. The next minute she was hoisting herself over the sill and plopping down into the room.

'Something wrong with the door?' he said.

'Yes – they won't let me use it! Sh!' She put a finger to her lips. 'It's all right so long as we talk quietly. I checked. Iris is out there, but she's half deaf.'

Was Iris, he wondered, the elderly nurse who

had been assigned to him in place of the over-sensitive Delian? If so, she wasn't much of an improvement. She had a face like a pinched arse, and she, too, treated him as if he were something that had crawled out of a cesspit.

'Why won't they let you in?' he said; though he knew the answer as soon as he asked the question. It was obvious, wasn't it? They thought he couldn't be trusted. Still, he was interested in April's explanation.

'They say you're not to be disturbed.'

'On what grounds?'

'Well, they *say* you need to rest. Do you need to rest?'

'I've been resting all day.'

'That's what I thought,' said April. 'I thought by now you'd probably be getting bored.'

'So what's the real reason?'

'Oh! Well, you know what they're like . . . fuss fuss fuss.'

'About what?'

'If you really want to know,' said April, busily not looking at him as she picked up the discarded essays and began leafing through them, 'they're scared that you'll get aggressive.'

Get aggressive; and what did that mean, he wondered?

'Are you scared I'll get aggressive?'

She looked at him consideringly, as if weighing up the possibility.

'I don't *think* so.'

'But you're obviously not sure.' So why, in that case, had she come? Female curiosity? He waved a hand towards the sheaf of papers. 'Do you really believe all that garbage?'

Doubtfully she said, 'Garbage?'

'Rubbish – junk – crap!' He reached across

and snatched them from her. She recoiled slightly, but fortunately didn't scream, as he realised, seconds too late, she might well have done. If they were really teaching them that all men had been thugs and sex maniacs it was hardly surprising they were on their guard.

'This!' He read from her own paper: '"In those days men were not trained and roamed the world in hordes, murdering and killing and causing havoc." And this' – written by some dumb trollop called Holly – '"Men used women for their own sexual gartification" – she can't even spell! – "not hesitating to be violent and abusive when they could not immediately get their own way." Crap! Arrant *crap*!' He sent the papers scattering across the bed.

April said, 'Sh!' and nodded towards the door.

'Well, but I've never heard such a load of drivel! Is this what they teach you?'

April drew up the chair and sat astride it, hooking her arms round the back and resting her chin on the bar. She gazed at him, solemnly, over the top.

'Don't you think it's true?'

'Do *you*?'

She was silent.

'Because if you do,' he said, 'what the plague are you doing sitting there?'

'I don't think maybe *all* men were like that. We have read of one or two who weren't. There was a man called Ghandi who wasn't. And a man called George Bernard Shaw. They refused to eat flesh and there is no record, as far as we know, of them abusing women. But I think obviously they must have been the exceptions.'

He stared at her. 'You actually believe that?'

'Well, we haven't made it up!' she retorted.

'It's all there, in the old books – books that were written by *men*, most of them. Why would they write things that weren't true?'

'Books are only stories,' he said.

'Not always.'

'But the world couldn't have functioned if men had done nothing but go round raping and murdering!'

'We never said that was *all* they did . . . just that a lot of them did it a lot of the time.'

He shook his head in disbelief.

'Are you telling me they didn't?' said April.

'A few may have done. Maybe a few always will. But they're the exceptions, not the rule! You can't treat all of us as sub-human just because of the odd one or two.'

'Odd one or two? Books are *full* of men doing the most disgusting things! In any case, we never treat anyone as sub-human. We're not sexist. We don't go round saying men can't do things because their brains are too small, which is what men used to go round saying about women.'

'No, you just effectively neuter them so they're neither one thing nor the other!' They were hissing at each other now, across the bed. 'It may be what you call civilised, but it's hardly very humane!'

'Men weren't very humane.'

'All right, so sometimes maybe some of them weren't! Does that make it acceptable for women to be inhumane in their turn?'

'It's not inhumane. All our men are perfectly happy.'

'Oh, are they? Is that really what you think? Tell me – ' he clawed, awkwardly, with his left hand, at the papers on the bed – 'do you know someone called David Tessa?'

'David. Yes.' She looked at him defensively. 'Why?'

'Read this and tell me if you think he's so happy!'

She took the paper and slowly read it through, frowning now and again as she did so. 'What makes you think he isn't?'

Irritably, he snatched it back. '"Women took what *then* appeared the only course open to them ... drastic if *seemingly* logical ... *alternative* methods of dealing with male aggression" ... does that strike you as written by someone who's perfectly happy at what you've done to him? What you call *training* ... that's a bit of a euphemism, isn't it? A nice word for a thoroughly nasty fact? I suppose you do actually know what happens? Or do they keep little girls in ignorance?'

She flushed, angrily. He'd thought that would get her. It would have got Patty, too.

'I'm not a little girl,' she said, 'and we are not kept in ignorance.'

'And you still go along with it?'

'I don't see,' she said, 'that it's anything so very terrible.'

'No? You try asking David Tessa! He'll tell you.'

That, for some reason, seemed to strike home. For the first time she appeared uneasy.

'And that's another thing,' he said. 'What's with all these ridiculous surnames?'

She said, almost abstractedly, 'What ridiculous surnames?'

'Tessa – Alison –'

'Alison was the w –'

'Yes, yes, I know all about Alison!' He said it

133

tetchily. He had had enough of being lectured by self-righteous females.

'I don't understand why you think they're ridiculous. Why shouldn't women have their own names for the first time in history?'

'What was wrong with the old ones?'

She drew herself up. 'What was wrong with them,' she said, 'was that they all belonged to men . . . they always came from the *father*.'

'So why not at least let the men keep their father's names?'

'Why should we?'

'Why shouldn't you?'

'We don't *have* fathers.'

'It's not a dirty word, you know. My sisters loved their father. It may surprise you to learn that they actually wept when he died. My mother, too.'

She set her jaw, stubbornly. 'All through history women have had to put up with male surnames . . . *Richard*son, *John*son — '

'Smith?'

'It was the men who were smiths!'

'Well, then, there's your answer. It was men who were active.'

'And what do you think the women were?' She spat it at him, venomously. 'You think they just sat around, doing nothing!? Is that what you think?'

'Watch it!' he said. 'I'm an invalid!'

April breathed, deeply and indignantly. 'I'm glad I didn't live in those days if that's what men were like.'

'What do you mean, if that's what men were like?'

'*Arrogant*,' she said.

He laughed. 'You should get together with

134

Patty! She's always accusing men of being arrogant.'

'Who's Patty? Is she one of your sisters?'

'The younger one.'

He noticed she didn't say 'your girlfriend?' Presumably the concept of boyfriend/girlfriend was unknown in this lunatic asylum. He had an urge to ask her about it, but before he could do so she had shot out of her seat and gone scudding back to the window.

'I must go! Meta will be wondering where I am.'

'You mean you didn't tell her?' He tutted disapprovingly. 'Black mark for you when she finds out! Hobnobbing with the enemy . . . Will she put you on report?'

'We don't *report* on each other,' said April. She opened the window and prepared to climb out. 'Did you read your Diary yet?'

'Yes, I did. Thank you.'

'Is it interesting?'

'It will be to my sisters. If you come and see me again,' said Daniel, 'I might let you look at it.'

'Is that a promise?'

'If you want it to be.'

'All right! I'll come tomorrow. Same time. Be ready to let me in.'

April jumped lightly to the ground and set off at a run towards the main gates. She had only meant to stop for a few seconds. She had left Meta in the refectory, having an argument with Linden about attitudes towards abortion in the late twentieth century. Linden held that abortion was something that had been imposed upon women by men, Meta said that if it hadn't been for men having no self-control and simply using women as receptacles, abortion would never have been necessary. Either way, they were agreed that it was the fault of men. It was the sort of argument they revelled in. With any luck they would still be at it.

April turned in at the door of the girls' house and headed for the stairs.

'What's the big rush?' said Holly.

Damn! Damn and bother and blast! If Holly were here, that probably meant that Meta and Linden were as well. As if reading her thoughts, Holly said, 'They're up in your room, still arguing. I've left them to it. I'm going down the Monkey Puzzle with Dell. Do you want to come?'

'Mm . . .' April hesitated. The Monkey Puzzle was the name of one of the big houses further along the road which the younger members of the community had recently taken over and refurbished for their own use as a club and general meeting place. There was music and dancing most evenings of the week. 'You go on,' said April. 'I might join you later.'

'It'll be more fun than sitting and listening to those two,' said Holly. 'Get on my nerves, they do.'

Holly bundled out through the front door, April went on up the stairs to the room she shared with Meta. Even as she opened the door she heard them: 'Yes, but it's still a woman's basic *right* – ' It was true that Linden and Meta did tend to go on rather.

'Where have you been?' said Meta. 'I thought you were coming straight back here?'

'I was talking to Holly.'

'Holly's only just left!'

'Yes, well, I got sidetracked. Before that – ' her brain whirred, frantically – 'I bumped into David.'

Linden raised an eyebrow. Meta said, 'David?'

'Yes. Have you spoken to him since he's been back?'

'We had a few words.'

'Did you think he sounded happy?'

Linden gave a short laugh. 'He ought to be! Working for Willow.'

'Oh, well, yes! I'm sure he's happy about that. But –'

'But what?' said Meta.

'I don't know, I just . . . oh, it doesn't matter! What are we going to do? Are we going down the Monkey Puzzle?'

Linden groaned. Meta said, 'Do you really want to?'

'Well, I don't just want to sit here all night!'

'No; all right.' Meta cast an apologetic glance at Linden. 'Are you going to come?'

'If I must,' said Linden.

April felt like saying, 'There aren't any rules that say you have to,' but on the other hand there was safety in numbers; with Linden there, Meta wasn't so likely to probe. She would have to think up some sort of excuse for tomorrow evening if she wanted to stay and have a proper talk. That was the trouble with living in such a close community, everybody always knew what everybody else was up to. It had never bothered her until now; but perhaps she had never until now wanted to do something which she knew would gain everyone's disapproval.

Well, it was their own fault. The most momentous event to occur in practically a hundred years, brought about almost single-handedly by April herself – because really, when it came to it, what help had Meta been? No help at all; only a hindrance – and they refused to let her participate! She had feared all along that Willow and Rowan would keep Daniel for themselves. Thought they were the only ones who could be trusted – the only ones who were capable of being *objective*. Wouldn't even let David in to see him, in spite of him having been chosen to work with Willow. It left one no option but to take matters into one's own hands.

David wouldn't, of course. He had always been the law-abiding one, April the one who rebelled. That was why it was so strange and disturbing, the essay he had written. Almost as if – as if he *regretted* that they were civilised. As if he knew that they had to be, but wished it wasn't necessary. Or that there was some other way.

He came into the Monkey Puzzle while April was dancing with Meta. He saw her and raised a hand in salute and she waved back at him, but could think of no excuse for going over to talk. After all, she was supposed to have talked to him already, wasn't she? She watched him, covertly, across the room. He was standing with a group of other boys – the same group, probably, as at the homecoming. He seemed to be joining in, laughing and talking with the rest of them, but he only stayed a few minutes and then turned as if to go.

April, by now, was sitting at a table in the corner with Meta and Linden. Holly had just come over, dragging Dell with her, to Linden's obvious annoyance. April craned her head, trying to see round Meta. David caught her gaze and smiled briefly at her before pushing through a crowd of people to the door. Again, she could think of no excuse for going after him.

This was ridiculous! Why would she need an excuse?

Abruptly, she pushed back her chair.

'I won't be a minute.'

'Why?' said Meta. 'Where are you –'

'Just want to say something to someone.'

April hurried out of the door, after David. He didn't hear her the first time she called. She had to call again, and this time he turned, and waited for her to catch up.

'Hallo,' he said.

'Hallo!' Now that she was here with him, she wasn't at all sure what she wanted to say. She could hardly ask him outright, are you happy?

'How are you?' she said.

If he were surprised by the question, he gave no sign of it. Gravely he said, 'I'm all right. How are you?'

'All right.'

She smiled. David smiled back.

'It's quite fun, isn't it?' She nodded towards the Monkey Puzzle.

'Yes; I don't remember it being there when I – went away.'

'It was only opened last year. We did it up ourselves.'

'I see. That was very enterprising.'

'Yes. I suppose it was.'

They stood, facing each other, enveloped in an awkward silence. Why was it all so complicated? thought April. This was *David*. Why couldn't she talk to him the way she used to?

'I was thinking, what you said the other day –'

'What was that?'

'About there being a – a gulf. Between us.'

'Between men and women; yes. I said that I

139

didn't remember it being like that. I realise now, of course, that it must have been, it's just that you don't notice these things when you're young. As you said, we're not children any more.'

'It's sad, though,' said April, 'in a way, isn't it?'

'It seems so to me,' said David. 'I thought to you it seemed quite natural?'

'Yes – well, I mean – I suppose it is, but it's still sad. That it has to happen.'

'Does it have to happen?'

'Well –'

'Who says that it has to?'

'No one actually *says*. It just . . . does. Doesn't it? I mean –'

She floundered; she was not used to these sort of discussions.

'We have to be civilised,' she pleaded.

'Oh, but of course!' There was a note of mockery in his voice. 'At all costs let us be civilised!'

'Well, but –'

From somewhere behind, Meta's voice, impatient, called, 'April! Where are you?'

'It sounds as if you're wanted,' said David.

'Yes.' She nodded, glad to be spared the embarrassment of attempting to explain something she was not sure she fully understood, yet at the same time reluctant to leave the matter unresolved. She sensed that to David it was important. 'We'll talk again?' she said.

'You know where to find me,' said David.

Meta was waiting for her at the top of the steps.

'Honestly,' she grumbled. 'You make me come

here, when I don't specially want to, then go running off to talk to David. I thought you'd already talked to him once?'

'I suppose there's no rule that says I can't talk to him again?'

Meta regarded her through narrowed eyes. 'You're starting to get very peculiar,' she said. 'Did you know that?'

April shrugged.

'It's what comes of being confined too long in one place ... I need a bit of *excitement* in my life.'

Chapter Nine

'I can stay longer tonight.' April swung her legs nimbly over the windowsill. 'Meta's gone to choir practice. I usually go with her, but I said I'd got a headache.' She settled herself, cross-legged, on the bed. 'Where's this Diary, then?'

'Is that the only reason you've come? To read the Diary?'

She looked at him, reproachfully. 'You promised!'

'Yes, and I'm keeping that promise! Here you are. Go ahead! Read it. I was just hoping – ' Daniel sat himself on the bed, next to her. April stiffened, but stayed where she was. (After all, she thought, I've only got to scream . . .) 'I was hoping,' said Daniel, 'that you might perhaps have come to see me as well as the Diary.'

'Oh, well, yes,' she said. 'I am interested in you, naturally.'

'The way you'd be interested in a prehistoric monster, no doubt.'

'I don't think of you as a monster,' she said.

'But you do think I'm pretty prehistoric?'

'Well – ' she hesitated.

'Of course you do! Don't try to spare my feelings. You all do. You make it quite obvious.'

'You see,' she said, 'you seem to us like someone from out of the past. I expect it was the same a hundred years ago when they found savage tribes still living in the jungle . . . they just couldn't believe that such people still existed.'

'You really know how to make a person feel good, don't you?' he said.

She eyed him, uncertainly. 'I didn't mean – I mean, I was only trying to –'

'Oh, don't take everything so seriously! Get on and read your Diary.'

He read it with her, over her shoulder, his arm brushing hers. It was his Diary, she couldn't very well ask him not to; but I have only to scream, she thought. And then after a while she grew used to it, and forgot about screaming, since he didn't seem to be going to jump on her. And really his presence wasn't as bad as all that.

They had discussed last night in the Monkey Puzzle, after Meta had dragged her back in, how it would feel to have a man – i.e., a primitive man – touch you. Meta had said it would be gruesome, like being clawed by a piece of old, hard leather. Linden, grandly, had declared herself above taking an interest in the matter, Holly and Dell had screwed up their faces and gone '*Eugh!* Horrible!'

April, sitting there amongst them, had felt strangely removed. She, after all, had been on her own with Daniel for almost two hours. She had talked to him. She had, actually, *touched* (if not been touched by) him. She couldn't feel quite the same hysterical revulsion as the others.

Meta had obviously sensed as much. She had looked directly at April and said, 'Never tell me you fancy the idea?' April had shuddered dramatically and squealed 'Eugh!' in faithful imitation of Holly, but she could tell Meta wasn't convinced. Well, that was too bad. She didn't enjoy having secrets from Meta, but this

143

might be the only chance she ever had to meet a real man as in pre-plague times.

'Are you finding it interesting?' said Daniel. She started, guiltily.

'Yes! It's fascinating!'

Friday 16th July. I am quite looking forward, now, to going away to camp. I was a bit scared at first, because of never having been away from home before, and I know Dad is still worried, but I've got to grow up some time!!! Simon Dobson went round the class this morning getting people to sign petitions to have water filters put on school drinking fountains. He is scared of aluminium making him go senile before he is twenty!

April shook her head. Small chance poor old Simon Dobson would ever have stood of even reaching twenty, the way things had turned out. She read on:

Saturday 17th July. Went shopping in the morning with Harry. Stayed in and painted in the afternoon.
Sunday 18th July. Saw Harry in the morning. Then stayed in and painted again.
Monday 19th July. Met Harry on the way to school. She has had her hair cut short for camp.

'Who is this Harry that she keeps talking about? I thought it was a boy, but she says she.'

'It was her best friend that she set off to go to Cornwall with. She seems to have been a bit of a liability . . . it says in the Journal that she ran away to go to a party.'

'A *party?* In the middle of a plague?'

144

'That's what it says . . . "Harry left to go to a party in Trafalgar Square." They never saw her again.'

'Sounds as if she was a bit looby.'

'Yes; that's the conclusion I came to.'

'So why is she called Harry? Isn't that a boy's name?'

'It's short for Harriet.'

'Oh.' April turned a page of the Diary. Carelessly she said, 'My great-grandmother was called Harriet. She was a bit looby.'

There was a silence.

'I suppose you don't know anything about her?' said Daniel.

'Only what it says in the records . . . she lived in Croydon and her family was dead and she was sixteen at the time of the plague. My great-grandmother was the only child she had. She went off scavving by herself one day and never came back. They think she must have had an accident . . . they found her remains,' said April, 'years later.'

'Frances Latimer was sixteen.' Daniel tapped the Diary. 'It says in there.'

They looked at each other.

'How extraordinary,' whispered April, 'if Harriet were Harry!'

'I suppose you don't know what her surname was? I suppose you didn't keep a note of surnames? Too sexist.'

'Actually, we did in those days. But I can't remember . . . it began with an S . . . Sa – Sum –'

'Somers?'

'Yes! That was it! Harriet Somers!'

'Take a look at this.' Daniel reached across and heaved his pack on to the bed. He dived his left hand down the side of it, emerging

145

triumphant with the Journal. 'Read that bit, there.'

'"For a short time my best friend, Harriet Somers" – it's her! It's Harriet!'

'This is extraordinary!' said Daniel. 'Clem's going to go wild when I tell her. She's always speculating about what could have happened to Harriet.'

'It makes us sort of linked,' said April, 'doesn't it? I wish I could tell Rowan! She'd go wild, too. You'll have to tell her.'

'Me?'

'Well, I can't, can I? I'm not supposed to have seen you.'

'No way!' He shook his head, vehemently. 'The less I have to do with their Royal Highnesses the better. They give me the creeping jinnies.'

'They won't do anything to you,' said April.

'That's what they *say*. But I sense a distinct frostiness . . . everyone except you treats me as if I were a running sore.'

'If you told Rowan about Harriet she'd be so excited she'd forget she was talking to a – 'April waved a hand.

'A running sore,' said Daniel.

'A danger to the community. She would! I bet you! Rowan gets very carried away by anything that's history. She might even let me come and talk to you, instead of having to keep climbing through the window.'

'You reckon?' said Daniel.

'Well, it's worth a try,' said April. 'And if you let them make a copy of it they'd be in your debt, and that's *got* to be a good thing.'

She knew next day that Daniel had done it.

Rowan came up to her in the refectory, where she was sitting as usual with Meta and the others.

'April,' she said, 'if you've finished, can I have a word with you?'

'Now what's she done?' said Meta.

Meta sounded suspicious – almost, thought April, as if she knew. But she couldn't possibly. She had still been at choir practice when April had arrived back last night.

'I'm sure she'll tell you all about it later,' said Rowan.

She hustled April out of the refectory and down the steps.

'Something rather exciting! You know the Diary which you and Meta retrieved for our guest? Well! You'll never believe it but I *think*, in fact I'm almost certain, that your great-grandmother Harriet appears in it! It seems our guest had noticed your name on one of the essays I gave him to read –'

Oh, clever! thought April. She had wondered how Daniel would explain having made the connection. She listened with suitable eagerness to the tale, making excited comments where she felt they were called for. She felt mean deceiving Rowan, but really it was their own fault. If Willow had let her in to see Daniel when she had asked, there would have been no need for all this deceit.

'Don't you think that's exciting?' said Rowan. 'Another bit of history fallen into place! And just in time for our Centenary! He's not only said that we can make a copy of it, he's actually given me his word that when he leaves we can keep his copy of the Journal. I'm really longing to get my hands on that!'

147

'That was nice of him,' said April, 'wasn't it?'

'I daresay he feels some kind of payment is due . . . considering if it hadn't been for us he'd almost certainly be dead by now – and he certainly wouldn't have the Diary!'

'All the same,' said April, 'he didn't have to let us, did he? He could just have kept it to himself.'

'Well – yes. I suppose.' Rowan looked at her. 'What are you trying to say?'

'Just that he can't be *all* bad. Though of course,' said April, hastily, 'I quite accept that he is a primitive male and must be treated with caution, but I do think, especially now that we've discovered about Harriet, that I ought to be allowed to go and read it.'

'You're absolutely right,' said Rowan. She crooked a finger. 'Come with me! We'll ask him if you can borrow it.'

It wasn't what she had intended, but what could she say? Meekly she went off with Rowan to the hospital. Demurely she entered the room at Rowan's side. Eyes cast modestly floorward, she waited whilst Rowan explained the purpose of their mission. Shyly she accepted the Diary from Daniel.

'I hope you find it interesting,' he said. His hand, as he gave it to her, touched hers. She was almost sure that it was done on purpose. She risked a quick glance upwards. With his back to Rowan, Daniel closed one eye in a wink. A giggle came bubbling up April's throat and had hastily to be turned into a choking fit.

'Do you want her to read it here or may she take it away with her?' said Rowan.

Daniel, still with his back turned, pulled a face. April quickly looked the other way.

'If you took it with you,' suggested Rowan,

'you could perhaps be the one to copy it out? Since you're the one it mainly concerns.'

A broad grin appeared on Daniel's face. April said, 'Maybe I should stay here and copy it?'

'Good heavens, I'm sure he doesn't think you're going to run off with it! He may have no very high opinion of us, but I don't believe we've given him any cause to distrust us?'

Daniel rolled his eyes.

'Have we?' said Rowan.

'No!' said Daniel. 'None at all. I sometimes wake up in the night and sweat a bit, wondering about the future generations I might never get to father, but apart from that – no! No cause whatsoever.'

'Well, there you are.' Rowan smiled. 'You can bring the Diary with you, April, and copy it out at your leisure – I think perhaps a thank you might be in order?'

April gazed up, meltingly, into Daniel's eyes.

'Thank you,' she breathed.

'Don't mention it,' murmured Daniel.

'She wouldn't let me come on my own.' April sprang down from the windowsill. 'I asked her, afterwards, and she said, "Out of the question, April. Don't be foolish. You're not a child any more."'

'And I gave her my word I wouldn't behave like a sex beast!'

'She obviously didn't believe you.'

'No, and if she finds you here she'll believe me even less!'

'She won't find me, she's working on the exhibition. Meta and Linden are helping her. I'm supposed to be sitting indoors copying out the blasted Diary.'

149

'What happens when they get back and find you haven't?'

'Oh! I'll say I had a headache, or got bored.'

He was silent a moment, watching her as she took up her favourite position, astride the chair.

'You know,' he said, 'that sooner or later they're going to find out, don't you?'

'What? About me coming to visit you?'

He nodded. She sat frowning, as she considered it.

'Why should they?'

'They always do.'

'Well, and so what?'

'It really doesn't bother you?'

'It doesn't bother *me*.' The look she threw at him was a challenge; virtually irresistible. 'Does it bother you?'

It ought to bother him. If he had a particle of sense he would send her packing right here and now. His mother always had said that girls would be the death of him.

'You know the expression playing with fire?' he said.

'Yes,' said April.

He grinned. 'There are times when it positively adds to the attraction . . .'

'Tell me about your sisters.' April curled up on the bed, her feet tucked beneath her. 'How old are they?'

'Clem's seventeen, Patty's just sixteen. And then there's Rick. But he's only a kid.'

She wasn't interested in Rick. She wanted to know about Patty and Clem.

'What are they like?'

'To look at? Or as people?'

'As people. Are they like us?'

'Patty is. I have a feeling she'd fit in very well with your mob.'

'Why's that?'

'She's what my mother calls a reb.'

'What does that mean?'

'It means she lives in a constant state of rebellion . . . thinks she ought to be allowed to do everything that boys do.'

April stiffened at once, indignantly. 'Why shouldn't she?'

'That's what she says.'

'And what do you say?'

'Me? I don't say anything. I keep well out of it!'

'*Coward.* If I came to live in your community I'd soon change things!'

'If you teamed up with Patty,' he agreed, 'you probably would.'

'What about Clem? What's she like?'

'Oh, Clem's a conformist. She likes things just the way they are. She wouldn't fit in here at all . . . she's being courted at the moment. She'll probably get wed quite soon.'

'Get *wed*?'

'Married,' he said. 'Like they did in the old days? One man, one woman –'

'That's *archaic*! Do you worship idols?'

'Oh, ar, ay!' He tugged at his forelock. 'We be a-goin' down on our knees reg'lar to the ole sun god an' the ole moon god . . . bit of the ole rain dance, bit of a knees-up, round the ole scrotum pole, doin' the ole fertility jig. We be havin' us a rare ole time!'

She stared at him, nonplussed. Obviously not accustomed to having her leg pulled. They did seem to take everything deathly seriously.

'What's a scrotum pole?' she said.

'Just my little dirty joke. Don't take any notice of it. You wouldn't know about such things in this place.'

'So, what does being courted mean?'

'It means going steady – boyfriend, girlfriend. Walking out together. Being a couple. Another thing you wouldn't know about.'

'We have couples,' said April.

'Boyfriends?'

'Girlfriends.'

'It's hardly the same.'

'So what's so wonderful about having a boyfriend?'

'Even if you haven't experienced it – ' it struck him, even as he said it, as being almost impossible – 'you must surely have read about it?'

'Yes, but I can never see what they got out of it.'

It was on the tip of his tongue to retort, 'That's because you've never met a real man!' He bit it back.

'It's hard to explain in words . . . I suppose it's the attraction of opposites. It is also,' he added, 'what nature intended.'

'If you're telling me nature intended women to be subjected and kept under and the world to be almost wiped out, then all I can say is, nature obviously needed to be improved upon!'

'Yes,' he said, 'you could well be right. But surely the answer is for women to become more assertive and not let themselves be subjected?'

'Why should we? We don't *want* to be more assertive!'

'That could be said to be socially irresponsible . . . you let men go on their way to destruction and do nothing to stop it.'

'Well, this time we have done something to stop it.'

'Yes, by virtually wiping out one half of the human race! Even if you say that men had it coming to them, just think of all the things you're missing out on.'

'What things?'

It was a temptation, again, to be glib. He resisted it.

'The fun,' he said. 'The sheer fun of it!'

'*Fun*? You call it *fun*? Being raped and murdered and –'

'Don't give me that! You know as well as I do it was hardly an everyday occurrence.'

Her face took on a mulish expression.

'Look, I'm not saying it didn't happen; just that it wasn't actually the norm, no matter what they tell you.'

'All right, then! So what's the fun of it? Fun of *what*?'

'Well . . . of being with the opposite sex.'

He waited for her to scream, or rush for the door.

'I suppose you're referring to *the act*,' she said.

'Not just that! There's far more to it than that!'

'There is?' She looked at him, doubtfully.

'Well, of course there is! You don't suppose men and women spent their lives together just because of that, do you?'

'No,' she said, promptly. 'Women were forced into staying with men because they were economically dependent on them. They got trapped.'

He shook his head, exasperated. 'You have been taught an extremely one-sided view of history.'

'Well, *weren't* they?' she said.

'It wasn't that simple! And even if it were, why do you suppose the men stayed with the women?'

She had the answer pat: 'Because they used them for sexual purposes.'

He groaned. 'I don't believe it! Who teaches you this load of junk?'

'Old books,' she said. 'And newspapers. I suppose you know what newspapers were? All about what was happening every day? And one of the things that was happening was that women were being raped. And if *that's* not using them for sexual purposes I'd like to know what is!'

'Don't you ever read any of the books about women who enjoyed it?' he said.

'Enjoyed being *raped*?'

'Enjoyed the company of men.'

'Oh! Well, some of them *say* they did.'

'So why would they say it if it wasn't true?'

For a moment that stumped her. 'I just can't imagine it,' she said, 'that's all.'

'You want me to show you?'

'No!' She backed away from him.

'I was only going to kiss you,' he said. 'Just so you'd know what it was like . . . wouldn't you like to know what it's like?'

April flung open the window.

'I'll think about it!' she said.

'You see?' said Daniel. 'It is quite fun, isn't it?'

April stared at him in wonderment, cheeks crimson, lips still bruised from the pressure of his mouth on hers. A week ago, she would have screamed the place down. Now she put up a hand, feeling herself.

'Does it show?'

'Of course it doesn't show! All I did was kiss you! Haven't you ever been kissed before?'

'Yes, but – ' Not like that. She couldn't decide whether she had liked it or not. She hadn't *dis*liked it. Meta was wrong about men feeling like old hard leather. They felt different from women, certainly; but that was only what you'd expect. They *were* different from women. She laughed, exultantly. If John and Fortune knew what she had been up to they would have apoplexies on the spot. Not only *alone* with a man, but *kissing* with a man . . . (She tried not to think, just for the moment, what Meta would say.)

'Did you feel that you were being used?' said Daniel. 'Suppose I put my arm round you – ' He did so. 'Does that feel as if you're being used?'

No, she thought; but there's more to it than that . . .

'What happened to your father?' she said.

'My father? He was killed at sea.'

'In a ship?'

'Fishing boat.' He said it without thinking. Instantly he could feel the disapproval creeping through her. She stiffened slightly in his arms.

'What does a fishing boat do?'

'It – um – catches fish,' he said.

'What for?'

There was a silence while he tried to think of some acceptable reason for catching fish.

'To eat them?'

'Well – yes. I'm afraid so.'

She breathed, deeply.

'It's traditional,' he pleaded. 'And anyway, you can't count fish. They're not animals.'

'They're living creatures,' said April. 'What

about your brother? What happened to him?'

'Philip? He was yobbed.'

'What's yobbed?'

'Set upon.'

Her brow wrinkled. It was obviously a concept she was not acquainted with.

'By what?'

'A couple of drunken louts in a dark alley. I suppose you're going to tell me – ' he tweaked at her hair – 'that you don't have drunken louts? Or dark alleys?'

Slowly she shook her head. 'What did they do it for?'

'The usual reason. He had something they wanted.'

'So they *killed* him?'

'They didn't actually mean to. But he put up a fight and – ' He hunched a shoulder. 'These things happen.'

She pursed her lips and fell silent.

'I know what you're thinking,' he said, 'you don't have to tell me. I don't pretend we've solved all our problems. But we are trying.'

She continued silent; plainly of the opinion that they still had a long way to go.

'It's hard to see, really,' she said at length, 'what advantages there are.'

'I'm an advantage,' he said, 'aren't I?'

'Go away!' She pushed at him, petulantly – almost, for a moment, like any other girl suddenly grown bored with male attentions. 'It must have been dreadful for your mother.'

'Yes.' He acknowledged it, soberly. 'Philip was her first born. He was always her favourite.'

'It seems such a *waste*.' Very hung up on waste they were, these women. 'And then you setting off . . . she must be worried half out of her mind, wondering if you're ever going to get back.'

'I wonder that myself, sometimes. If they were to find out what you and I are up to —'

'We're not *up* to anything.' She corrected him, sternly. 'I'm conducting research.'

'Oh! Is that what you're doing? So what am I doing?'

'You're helping me — you're the subject of my research.'

'Is that all?'

'Yes!' She slapped at him. 'Stop doing that, I've had enough research for tonight. I ought to be going, or Meta will be back.'

'Wait!' He caught at her as she made to do her usual disappearing act through the window. 'You ought to have just one more small piece of research before you go . . . when members of the opposite sex say goodbye at the end of an evening, they always exchange kisses.'

'Do they?'

'Take it from me,' he said.

'We'll have to exchange them quickly then, because I really must be going.'

'The merest peck —'

Dutifully, April tilted her face towards him. She thought, I am becoming quite accomplished . . . in future when she read books about people from the past she would know a bit better what they were talking about.

She swung herself over the sill and set off at a lope towards the gates. As she did so, a figure stepped out of the shadows. It was almost as if he had been waiting there for her.

'Had a good evening with your boyfriend?' said David.

Chapter Ten

'I wasn't spying on you! I realise it looks that way, but –'

There was a pause. April stood, waiting. He ran a hand through his hair, obviously embarrassed.

'You're not the only one who's got an interest.'

She couldn't immediately understand what he meant.

'I can assure you,' he muttered, 'that my curiosity is at least as great as yours.'

'You want to talk to Daniel?'

'Does that strike you as odd?'

'No! I still can't see why they won't let you. I can see why they won't let *us* –'

'Actually they did let me,' said David, 'for about five minutes. I was sent as ambassador . . . the token male who's done so well for himself.'

'Well, but you have!' agreed April. 'Working with *Willow* . . . Linden's positively green!'

'Oh, I'm sure.'

'She is! Honestly!'

'You think she'd like to change places?'

'She'd do *anything*.'

'Not quite anything,' said David.

There was a pause.

'Well, anyway,' said April, 'at least you've seen him.'

'And been kept very well away ever since!'

'What are they so scared of? I don't see what

they're scared of! Do they think he'll turn violent, or something?'

He gave a short laugh. 'More likely think I will.'

'You?'

'Yes – me!' His lip curled, in self-derision. 'Ludicrous, isn't it?'

'It's idiotic!' said April. She said it indignantly. Violence was almost unknown in the community, and David, especially, was the last person to be capable of it. Even as a small boy he had been quiet and contained. It had been April who had got into all the fights, not David. 'What do they think you'd be violent for?'

He walked a few paces with her before replying.

'Envy,' he said, 'can turn people very spiteful.'

It took a few moments for the full import of his words to sink in. She remembered John and the kitchen knife. She looked at David in consternation.

'Oh, don't worry,' he said. 'I've no desire to curtail his pleasures, even if I could. My interest is a purely intellectual one. It's all it can be really, isn't it? When you think about it.'

'In that case – ' she said it quite seriously – 'why not go to Willow and tell her? *Say* that your interest is purely intellectual. Say that you just want to discuss things.'

'I've already suggested it.'

'And she said no?'

'She said it would have to be a community decision.'

'Yes, that's what she always says when she wants to stop you doing something and can't find a good reason for it. And then we have a meeting and everybody talks and in the end they all do whatever she wants them to do.'

He frowned. 'Is that democratic?'

'I suppose so.' April hunched a shoulder. She wasn't particularly interested in the political workings of society. 'Everybody gets their chance to say something.'

'But they all do what Willow wants?'

'Usually.' He shook his head. 'I still don't see,' said April, 'what she's got against you talking to him.'

'Talking is just about the last thing she'd want me to do . . . who needs disaffection in the ranks?'

'Are you saying – ' April sought for the right words as they walked together through the main gates. She wasn't sure how to put it. She didn't want to make any mistakes, or unintentionally insult him. 'Are you saying that if you talked to Daniel it would – '

'Make me dissatisfied with my lot? Yes. I should think it very well might, wouldn't you?'

She was troubled. It was not something she had ever considered.

'I thought most people just . . . took it for granted.'

'One certainly isn't given much choice in the matter, if that's what you mean.'

'You think people ought to be given a choice?'

'Don't you?'

She rubbed the bridge of her nose. 'If you had had one – '

'I'd probably still have gone along with it, the same as the rest of them. A choice at that age isn't necessarily any choice at all. You just do what you're told, because it's expected of you. Because everyone else does it. It's only since – coming back and – remembering . . . the way things used to be – '

She looked at him, shyly. 'Does it really bother you so much?'

'What do you think? Now that you've been with *him*? Now that you know – ' again, his lip curled – 'what men are supposed to be like?'

Swiftly she said, 'He's not that different from you!'

'No? I can't see you kissing me that way.'

A tide of red engulfed her cheeks. 'Would you want me to?'

'Oh!' He hunched a shoulder, and began abruptly to walk on. 'What would be the point?'

'I will,' she said, 'if you like.'

David stopped. He rounded on her, savagely. 'Don't you patronise me, April!'

'I wasn't! Truly! I didn't mean – '

'No! You never do mean, do you? Any of you!'

Chastened, she walked in silence at his side.

'I read your essay,' she said at last, rather timidly.

He grunted.

'Rowan gave it to Daniel to read. She gave him mine, as well. He said mine was a load of crap. Then he showed me yours.'

'No comment.'

'Do you really think there could be another way of managing things?'

'There's got to be a better way than this.'

'But whenever we've had debates about it, it's always been you – well, the others. John and the others – who've said we can't afford to let male aggression dominate us again.'

'Don't you think by now that women have enough confidence to deal with that and not let it happen?'

She was doubtful. 'Mm . . .'

'Can you honestly imagine women like Rowan and Willow – or Meta and Linden – ever letting men push them around again?'

'What about me?'

'I don't know about you. You're a bit more problematic; you're not as hard-edged. But with the Rowans and the Willows to lead the way, you'd stand firm. It's silly little mutts like Dell and Holly who might revert. But society could cope with that – just as it could cope with the few men who gave them problems. After a hundred years? It ought to be able to!'

'You know what you ought to do,' said April. 'You ought to speak at the next debate.'

'I'll speak, but I shan't get anywhere. All that will happen is that I shall make myself unpopular.'

'Suffragettes used to be unpopular.'

'Yes, but at least there was more than one of them!'

'I'll support you,' said April.

'Then you'll be unpopular, as well.'

'So that would make two of us.' She rose quickly on tiptoe and touched his cheek lightly with her lips. 'Two's better than one and we always used to do things together!'

By the time she reached their room Meta was back from choir practice, sitting on the bed painting her toenails yellow ochre.

'That won't stay on more than five minutes,' said April.

'So? I suppose I can do it if I want to do it?'

April shrugged. It wasn't like Meta to make childish retorts.

'Anyway, I thought you'd got another headache?'

'I did. I went for a walk to get rid of it.'

Meta looked at her from under her lashes.

'I'd have been back earlier, only I was talking to David.'

'Again?'

'He's going to speak at the next debate . . . he's going to say it's about time we stopped doing what we do to men.'

Meta raised an eyebrow.

'He thinks after a hundred years we ought to have learnt how to cope with them and not let them get the better of us. I'm going to support him,' said April.

'Oh. Really?' said Meta.

'Yes; I don't think it's right. It might have been *then*, but I don't think it is now.'

'What's brought this on all of a sudden?'

'Talking to David. I told you he wasn't happy. And it's awful because he didn't have any choice and now it's been done and he's got to stay like that for the rest of his life and I don't think we have any right. I think we *would* have a right if a man was aggressive, but I think we ought at least to give them a fair chance.'

'Sentimental claptrap!' Meta waved a foot in the air. 'Are you sure this isn't something to do with *him*?'

'Sorry?' said April. 'I don't know anyone called him.'

'The ape!' snapped Meta. 'The barbarian!'

'If you mean Daniel, why not say so? It's extremely rude,' said April, 'not to refer to people by their names.'

'I'm not sure that I regard him as a person.'

'Well, you ought!'

'Why ought I? Give me one good reason.'

'Because he *is* a person! He's got feelings just the same as the rest of us.'

'I doubt that,' said Meta. 'And anyway, how do you know?'

'Because he told me!'

'Told you he'd got feelings?'

'Told me about his family. He's got a mother and two sisters that he really cares about, and he's had a lot of unhappiness in his life. His father died at sea and his elder brother was killed by drunken louts, and he's just as capable of suffering as we are.'

'Is that so?' Slowly Meta raised her head to look at her. 'How very interesting. Thank you so much for telling me.'

They went to bed that night thoroughly disgruntled with each other. Meta said, 'You see what happens when there are men . . . they ruin everything. They can't help it, they're just naturally destructive.'

April dreamt that night about Daniel. He looked like David, but she knew that he was Daniel. It was rather disturbing.

'Why don't you come with me?' murmured Daniel.

'To Cornwall?'

'Mm . . .'

April twisted in his arms to look at him. 'What would I do there?'

'Well, you could marry me, for a start –'

'*Marry* you?'

'We'd have to be married,' he said, 'if we wanted to live together. We're a very moral bunch. Not like you lot. I know it's quaint and old-fashioned, but my poor Ma would have a fit if we weren't all legal and above board.'

'But I'm an outsider,' said April. 'Wouldn't she mind?'

'She wouldn't, if you didn't. And just think what you and Patty could do together . . . we'd all be vegetarian feminists in no time!'

April thought; not about what she and Patty could do together, but what she and Daniel might . . . her heart thudded alarmingly against her ribs.

'How about it?' He brushed his cheek against hers. 'Would they let you?'

'Oh, they'd *let* me.'

They were not a repressive society: everybody was free to do whatever she wished, so long as it wasn't anti-social. She had no doubts on that score. In fact, she wasn't sure that she had doubts on any score. She would miss Meta horribly, but after last night she was seriously beginning to wonder whether she and Meta were right for each other. And the chance to travel – to see another place, other people – the chance to be with Daniel –

Of course, there was David. She had forgotten about David. She was stricken with a momentary pang. She had given him her promise of support. But surely he wouldn't expect her to forgo such an opportunity only for that? After all, they both knew that whatever motion he put forward didn't have a hope of being adopted. Not this time, not next time, not the time after that. Maybe not even in their lifetimes at all. He wouldn't ask that sacrifice of her. Would he?

'What do you reckon?' Daniel nuzzled at her. 'Could you stand the thought of living amongst primitives?'

'It's not so much that I mind you being primitives –'

'As what?'

She swallowed. He tilted her chin. 'What is it that you mind?'

'You see,' she whispered, 'I promised David . . .'

'David? The one who wrote the essay?'

She nodded.

'What did you promise him?'

'I promised that I'd help him fight . . . to get things changed.'

He said grimly, 'I'm glad someone round here thinks it's time things were changed. But I have to say . . . what good would it do David? Now?'

She bit her lip.

'Listen.' He took her by the shoulders. 'Be realistic! Think of yourself. It's too late for David. The tragedy's already happened – his life's already been ruined. Yours is still ahead of you! Do you really want to miss out on all the things nature intended?'

'But David –'

'Forget David! David's going to miss out whether you stay or not. There isn't anything he can do for you. He can't give you what I can give you. OK! So that's tough, I feel for him, b –'

Daniel broke off as there came the sound of a key turning in the lock. April scrambled instantly to her feet and made for her bolthole, but already the door was opening.

'April.' It was Willow's voice; very calm and cool. It expressed no surprise at finding her there. 'Please don't climb out of the window. It really isn't very dignified.'

She held the door open: April had no option but to go through it. In a low voice, as she passed, Willow said, 'Wait in my office. I want a word with you.' She wasn't even able to exchange a last glance with Daniel.

Willow followed her out, pausing only to lock the door of Daniel's room and pocket the key.

'You do realise,' she said – she perched on the edge of her desk and folded her arms across her chest – 'that your irresponsible behaviour is liable not only to make things very difficult for me but to put Daniel's safety at risk?'

The colour rushed confusedly to April's cheeks.

'I have given him my word,' said Willow, 'that he will not be touched. If the news gets out that you have been secretly visiting him, matters may well be taken out of my hands. I can't dictate to the rest of the community. Any promise that I have personally given is quite capable of being overruled. You never thought of that, I suppose, did you? You never do think of things, April, do you?'

'All I've been doing,' said April, 'is just talking to him!'

'I'm prepared to believe you. Others, however, may not be.'

'I don't really see what it has to do with anyone else!'

Willow sighed. 'What it has to do with anyone else, April, is the simple fact that we are a community. We can't act in isolation one from another. You know as well as I do that Daniel's presence amongst us faces us with a very real problem. We're dealing with that problem as best we can. We have no wish to harm him, but equally we have to make sure that he's in no position to harm us. For both his sake and for ours it's been thought wisest to keep him in isolation until such time as he's fit to leave. Until then, however, I am expecting you to behave sensibly. You'll be allowed the opportunity to say goodbye. In the meantime I should like to think I can trust you.

'So please, April, do not do it again. I can't forbid you, but I am appealing to you. For everyone's sake. Just go away now and think about it.'

April walked slowly across to the door. There she turned.

'Did someone tell you?' she said.

'That you were getting in to see him? Someone alerted me to the possibility, yes. I'm very grateful that they did, and so should you be. It shows a proper perception of the dangers you were running.'

David. It could only be David. He was the only person who had known. She felt a sharp stab of disappointment. David, of all people! David, who had been her friend, almost as close as Meta . . . how could he do such a thing? And after she had promised him her support! His betrayal was more wounding than any of Willow's strictures. She had trusted him, and he had let her down. She truly would not have thought it of him. What was it he had said? Something about envy making people spiteful . . . had he been trying to warn her what he was planning to do? Had he been planning it all along, even while she was pledging her support?

Hurt tears drenched her eyes. She brushed them away, angrily. It was bad, what they had done to David, but he didn't have to take it out on her. She had been prepared to fight with him, to stand by him, even, if necessary, make herself unpopular with the rest of the community. She was his one ally; he oughtn't to treat her like this.

'April!' Dell and her gang descended on her as she turned up the road towards the girls' house. 'We're going down the Monkey Puzzle. Coming?'

April shook her head. She wasn't in the mood for jollity.

'Oh, come on! Have some fun for once!'

They tugged at her, trying to drag her along with them. Irritably, she pushed them off.

'Get away!'

She didn't want mindless noise and activity; she wanted to creep into bed, by herself, in the dark with the curtains closed, and nurse the wound of David's betrayal. Their voices, shrill and aggrieved, pursued her up the road.

'Prune features!'

'What's she so sour about?'

'Oh, leave her! If she wants to be miserable, that's her problem.'

She didn't *want* to be miserable; no one *wanted* to be miserable. There were times when you just couldn't help it.

'April assures me,' said Willow, 'that you have only been talking.'

'She assures you quite correctly.'

'I don't doubt it for a moment. I hardly imagined,' said Willow, crisply, 'that you would abuse our hospitality by taking advantage of a rather foolish and trusting young woman – for whose behaviour I can only apologise, by the way.'

'There's no need to apologise. April's been the only thing that's kept me sane.'

An eyebrow went up. 'Oh?'

'You probably don't have any such institution in your wonderful society as a prison –'

'Quite right,' said Willow. 'We don't.'

'Well, being less than perfect we do. However, I'm here to tell you that even our prisoners get to communicate more than I've communicated these past couple of weeks!'

'Are you complaining about our treatment of you?'

'You saved my life, and for that I'm grateful. You've also fed me, and for that I'm also grateful. But I do object to being shut away as if I'm some kind of – of disease!'

'I have explained twice already,' said Willow, 'that it is entirely in your own interests.'

'Why? What are they out there? A gang of uncontrollable maniacs? All these *civilised people* . . . or is it that you're scared I might put a few inconvenient notions into their heads?'

'I can assure you,' said Willow, smoothly, 'that that is something I am not in the least bit scared of.'

'In that case, why can't I be allowed to talk to them? If I'm willing to take the risk –'

'You want to try converting them to your way of thinking?'

'If you're so convinced you've got right on your side, what have you got to lose?'

'I personally,' said Willow, 'have got nothing to lose.' She smiled at him, rather sweetly. Was she being humorous? If so, it was the first spark he had seen. 'Very well.' She stood up. 'If you really insist I'll call a meeting for tomorrow night. You can address the whole community. Never let it be said that we stifled free speech.'

Sanctimonious! thought Daniel. They were all so damned sanctimonious.

Chapter Eleven

'As I am sure you all know – ' Willow stood on the platform, addressing a crowded hall. Daniel stood beside her, trying to locate April and Meta amongst the sea of faces. Meta, he thought, could be trouble – 'for the past couple of weeks we have had a guest staying with us. He has come from the outside – by boat. Isn't that right?' He dipped his head. 'Sailing all the way round the coast from Cornwall and up the Thames as far as London, then walking the rest of the way. A feat,' said Willow, 'not only of great endurance but great courage, also. I think you will agree.'

The audience dutifully murmured and shuffled their feet. At least she was prepared to be generous; he would give her that. But then, he thought, she could afford to be: she was on her home ground.

'The purpose of his visit, as doubtless some of you will have heard, was to retrieve a diary written by his great-grandmother, Frances Latimer, who made the journey from Croydon to Cornwall at the time of the plague. One of the people she made the journey with became our guest's great-grandfather – ' did he notice a slight uneasy twitching on the word grandfather, or was he imagining it? – 'the other dropped out and came back to Croydon, where she was one of the founder members of our community. She was Harriet.'

Definite tremors at that. Their interest in their own personal history seemed boundless. Not so interested in anything outside it.

'Our guest has very kindly allowed us to make a copy of the Diary, so that it will be available for everyone to read. He has also most generously promised to leave us his personal copy of Frances Latimer's Journal, which she wrote at the time of the plague. In return, he has requested that he be allowed to tell us something about his community and how it differs from ours. The very fact that the hall is so full would seem to indicate that we're all eager to learn. I'm sure at the end, if you have any questions, our guest will be only too happy to answer them.'

Again, he nodded. He had just caught sight of April, sitting near the front. She had grinned at him and held up her hand, palm outwards, in what he took to be a sign of encouragement. He could do with a bit of encouragement. He was aware of a tension in the atmosphere, of an underlying hostility, row upon row of eyes intently watching him. He could see Rowan, sitting centre front; he hadn't yet located Meta.

'Right. Well – ' Willow stepped aside, graciously waving him forward. 'I'll leave the floor to you.'

Suddenly he spotted her, at the end of the front row, next to a girl with long honey-coloured hair. He just knew there was going to be trouble from that quarter. He bet she was storing up the questions even now . . . 'Isn't it true that you eat flesh? Isn't it a fact that you carry firearms?'

He angled himself away from her, addressing

his words to the more friendly section of the audience which contained April.

'I'd like to start off by expressing my thanks to the community as a whole for saving my life.' Good manners, his mother always said, never hurt anyone. 'I was warned before I left home that I might encounter anything from head hunters to cannibals –'

Pause for laugh, which didn't come. Too late, he remembered that with his flesh-eating habits they probably regarded him as little better than a cannibal. *Clang*. Never mind. Press on.

'Nobody ever considered the possibility that I might have the great good fortune to come across people who were prepared to take me in and feed me.'

Did he, out of the corner of his eye, see Rowan furiously scribbling something on a scrap of paper?

'Really why I wanted this opportunity to talk to you, apart from saying thank you, was not so much to point up the differences in our communities as to emphasise the similarities.'

Shifting of bums on seats. They didn't want to hear about the similarities. Well, they were damn well going to.

'One thing that's struck me,' said Daniel, 'while I've been here, is that people tend to shy away from me – as if perhaps they think I'm not quite human.'

More shifting. Several throat clearings. General embarrassment. Serve them right. It was about time they heard the truth.

'Well,' he said, 'I am human. Just as human as the rest of you. And in spite of having the misfortune to be born the wrong sex –' sharp intakes of breath. And this time Rowan really was scribbling furiously – 'in spite of that,' said Daniel, 'I can assure you that I have never raped anyone, never murdered anyone, never, so far as I'm aware, physically harmed anyone – unless you count giving my brother a black eye at the age of ten, but I have to say that that is nothing compared with what one of my sisters once gave *me.*'

Stony silence. Did these people have no sense of humour?

All right; forget the humour. Give it them straight.

He gave it them straight; telling them in detail about his family – about his mother, weeping over the deaths of his father and Philip, and now waiting anxiously at home for him to return; about ten-year-old Rick declaring himself 'the man of the family' (that didn't go down well, but sod 'em), about Clem being courted and Patty wanting to come with him – scribble scribble, went Rowan, on her scrap of paper. He told them about the Journal, how it had been handed down through the generations: how Clem knew it almost by heart, how she had made him a copy to take with him on his travels, how it was for her, more than anyone, that he had wanted to find the Diary – and how in the end it had been April and Meta who had found it for him.

At the mention of April and Meta he could see heads turning, trying to pinpoint the two of them. He hoped he hadn't done them a disservice by naming them. Far from becoming less hostile, the atmosphere had, if anything, grown more so as he talked. He had never addressed a large audience before, but he didn't need to be experienced to know that he was not winning them over.

'Well – ' He shrugged his shoulders. 'What more can I say? If that hasn't proved that in spite of our differences we are very much the same –'

Willow stepped forward; cool and poised. The very essence of benevolence.

'I should like to thank our guest,' said Willow. 'I'm sure we all found what he had to say extremely interesting. Does anyone have any questions? Yes! Rowan?'

Rowan stood up. 'You started off by saying – ' she glanced at her scrap of paper – 'that nobody ever considered the possibility you might come across people who would be prepared to take you in and feed you. Does that mean that your community would not take in and feed a stranger were she in need?'

Damn the woman.

'I was only trying to be polite,' he said. 'No, it does not mean that.'

'But the implication is that you are suspicious of strangers.'

'Aren't you?' he countered. 'Haven't I been kept in isolation for that very reason?'

'That – ' she came back with it, smoothly – 'is not because you're a stranger but because, as you yourself pointed out, you had the misfortune to be born the wrong sex.'

'Oh! So you admit it's a misfortune?'

'I was quoting you. *You* seem to feel it's a misfortune.'

'In this community it all too obviously is.'

Sharp hisses. Agitated scuffling. Willow said, 'Sorrel?'

A striking woman with a mane of long tawny hair stood up.

'I should like to know how your society is run. Do you call yourselves a democracy?'

'We don't call ourselves anything.'

'So how do you organise?'

'We have a council.'

'Elected?'

'Of course.'

'Does everyone have a vote?'

'Everyone over a certain age.'

'And what does this council do? Does it lay down rules?'

'It decides how the community should function.'

Willow broke in. 'Yes! Fortune?'

An aged crone spoke from the sidelines. 'What proportion of women do you have on this council?'

Of course he had known someone was going to ask that. He wondered whether to lie about it, but saw no reason for doing so.

'Women don't stand for the council.'

Willow had to raise both hands to silence the uproar.

'There is a reason for that –'

'Oh, I'm sure!' cried a voice from the back of the hall. 'Male domination, that's the reason!'

'The reason – ' Daniel shouted over the hubbub – 'is that women prefer to occupy themselves with domestic matters. It's their own choice entirely.'

'Oh, is it?' Sorrel was on her feet again. 'Suppose a woman decided that she wanted to stand? Would she be allowed?'

'There aren't any rules which say she couldn't, but I doubt if anyone would vote for her. In our society,' said Daniel, 'we recognise a basic fact of nature: men and women may be

176

equal, but they are different.'

More uproar. Cries, jeers, catcalls. Another woman was on her feet. Old, but imposing: tall, dignified, white hair.

'Linnet,' said Willow.

'I just wanted to ask our guest,' said Linnet, 'how men and women can be called equal when it's men who do all the laying down of the law?'

'They're voted in for that purpose.'

'And you wouldn't suppose that being men they have mainly men's interests at heart?'

'Not at all. Women represent fifty per cent of the community; it wouldn't make sense to run it only for the other fifty per cent.'

Someone shouted, 'Oh, no?' Someone else shrieked, 'Rubbish!' He tried to imagine his mother or Clem yelling and bawling at a public meeting; he couldn't. He didn't think he would want to. Patty just might be bold enough to open her mouth, but she'd get a clip round the ear the minute she got home.

Willow pointed. 'Rowan?'

Rowan was already up on her feet again.

'You said your sister wanted to come with you and help find the Diary. Why wasn't she allowed to?'

'She's only sixteen,' said Daniel.

'You mean, she's too young to face possible danger? Would she still have been too young if she were a boy?'

He shrugged.

'Yes,' said Rowan. 'Or no?'

'Possibly not.'

'I see. On what grounds? That boys, perhaps, are tougher than girls? I wonder if you realise that April and Meta are only sixteen? And that retrieving the Diary for you involved considerably more than simply walking into a house and taking it?'

'I did realise and I'm extremely grateful to them, but I would never have asked it of them. It was their own choice.'

'Just as it was your sister's choice to accompany you!'

Stiffly he said: 'Where I come from we consider it a man's job to face danger, not a woman's.'

An angry roaring filled the hall. Some daffy-looking blonde was up on her feet, screaming.

'Who are you to dictate who does what?'

Irritated, he snapped, 'I don't *dictate*!'

'So why wasn't she allowed to come with you? If that was her choice?'

'She was allowed to put her case to the council. That's as much as anyone can do, male or female.'

'But the council are all men!'

'If women vote for us, is that our fault?'

'Yes, if you keep them in ignorance. If y – '

'All right, Dell, let someone else . . . Fortune?'

The aged crone spoke again.

'Back at the start of the twentieth century women wrested the right to vote from a male stranglehold. Theoretically that gave them equality with men. In practice it did nothing of the kind. Men still continued to wield all the power.'

'Well, listen to what you're saying!' said Daniel. 'Why did they? That's what you've got to ask yourself. The answer seems to me quite plain – they were more suited to it!'

'That may very well be true.' Rowan broke in without waiting to be asked. The furious upsurge provoked by his words died down at the sound of her voice. 'It may indeed be true, which is precisely the reason we took steps to curb male dominance in the first place – because we have no desire to have people wielding power. Power is a corruption, and any society which operates from a power base is a corrupt society.'

He felt like saying 'Crap!' but managed to restrain himself.

'That,' he said curtly, 'is a corruption in itself.'

'Oh, is it? Well, let me tell you – ' A flabby, spongelike creature was dancing in front of him, waving its arms and shaking with barely suppressed rage.

Willow gestured towards him. 'John?'

'Let me tell you that male aggression is something we cannot afford to have unleashed upon the world a second time! Men cannot control their baser instincts. They have to be controlled for us. The power of the male is a force for evil, bringing destructon on the world.'

Just bite your tongue, thought Daniel.

'Not, surely,' he said, 'if it's channelled constructively?'

'You can't channel it constructively! It won't allow itself to be channelled! It only breaks out again. And when it breaks out it has twice the force it had before, from being pent up.'

'Yes! David,' said Willow.

David Tessa stood up. He recognised him by his blond hair.

'I'd just like to say that I don't necessarily agree with John. I think in a society which has a sound traditon of democracy – not the so-called democracy of the twentieth century, but true democracy, without power bases, as we have here – then male aggression could almost certainly be channelled constructively . . . there is such a thing as creative energy. It doesn't necessarily have to be destructive.'

'Right!' Daniel seized on it, gratefully. 'As witness all the great works of the past. Westminster Abbey, the Pyramids, the –'

'The nuclear bomb? Chemical weapons? The plague?'

Meta. He had known she wouldn't be able to keep out of it for long.

'Those were the result of male aggression *not* being channelled constructively.'

'So what is the carrying of weapons the result of?'

'Self-protection.'

Ironic jeers rang through the hall.

'You call it self-protection –' An elfin child with close black curls was up and bawling at him.

'Holly?' said Willow.

'He calls it *self-protection* to kill other life forms?'

'Never mind other life forms,' retorted Meta, 'they go round killing *each other*!'

That incensed him. 'We do no such thing!'

'No? Then tell us how your brother died!'

She stood there, challenging him. He swallowed.

'Philip's death was an accident.'

'Yes – he was murdered by drunken louts. With their bare hands or with weapons? Not that it really matters. It's still male aggression.'

Someone he recognised as Delian, his reluctant carer from the first day, was waving his hand.

'Yes. Delian,' said Willow.

'We've not had one death by violence in the whole history of this community. We don't want to start now.'

He seemed to be addressing himself more to the boy called David than to Daniel. 'Our women can go in safety, without fear of being molested. We all work together for the common good. Speaking for myself, I'd like to keep it that way.'

A loud chorus of assent greeted this personal declaration. Delian sat down, looking smugly self-satisfied.

'Were you allowed to speak for yourself originally?' said Daniel.

'Originally when?'

'When you were – however old you were. Fourteen? Fifteen? Were you given any choice in what happened to you? Were you allowed any say in the matter? Or was it decided for you – by a bunch of women?'

Indignation he had been prepared for. The cacophany which followed was more than mere indignation. More, even, than antagonism. All over the hall people were out of their chairs, shrieking and yelling. Insults and invectives filled the air. The content of some was decidedly unpleasant.

'Everybody – please!' Willow positioned herself just slightly in front of him. She held up a hand for silence. Surprisingly, the hubbub died down, became a muted mumbling of discontent. 'I think the least we can do is give our guest the chance to reply.'

He shook his head. 'I have no more to add. You're condemned out of your own mouths . . . who's being aggressive? Not me!'

'Unwise,' murmured Willow, as the howling started up again. The girl with the honey-blonde hair, sitting next to Meta, was waving her arms. Willow nodded in her direction.

'Linden?'

She rose to her feet. Her face was tense and drawn, her body shaken by tremors. Nerves? Or suppressed anger?

'There is a difference – ' her voice sliced, cold and sharp, like a knife through the air – 'between verbal aggression and physical. We are not the ones who go round raping and murdering. We may reserve the right to attack you in words, but what we will never do, unless you raise your hand against us, is offer you physical violence.'

He was staggered by the bold-faced effrontery of it.

'What about them?' He flung out an arm, embracing Delian and the sour-faced John and a group of others sitting at one side of the hall. 'You offered them physical violence, didn't you? At an age when they were too young to defend themselves. At least in the past women had a chance to fight back, if they'd cared to take it – these poor fools don't! You seem to have maimed their brains as well as their bodies!'

There was a momentary pause; and then all hell broke loose.

'I think,' murmured Willow, 'we had better make a discreet exit . . .'

Chapter Twelve

'I'm sorry,' said Willow, 'that they gave you such a rough time.'

Patronising bitch.

'You obviously have them very well trained,' said Daniel.

'I told you,' said Willow. 'They're happy.'

'Yes, like animals . . . mindlessly!'

She shrugged.

'And what about the only one who dared to speak out – the only one who had the guts . . . David. You think he's happy?'

'David. No.' A faint cloud passed across the clear sky of her complacency. 'With someone like David . . . it's regrettable. Unfortunately one can't afford to make exceptions.'

'So he's condemned to a half life, for the sins of his fathers?'

'When the sins of his fathers had such hideous consequences, what would you suggest?'

'But how long does it go on?' he cried. 'A vendetta till the end of time?'

Irritation creased the smooth brow. 'It's not a question of a vendetta. That would be petty and indefensible. We are simply trying to apply the lessons of the past.'

'In isolation from the rest of the world? What is that likely to achieve?'

'All we can do is set an example. Whether future generations choose to follow our way or revert to yours is up to them. When you go back to your own people – and I think in the circumstances it might be wise if we arrange for you to slip away early tomorrow morning. We will of course give you provisions for your journey, and transport as far as the end of the valley. I'll trust you to let the horse go at that point: it will find its own way home. When you are back, I'm hoping that you will not condemn us out of hand. I do realise that the temptation will be there. But if I am willing to accept that our ... arrangements might strike you as extreme, I think perhaps you might accept that there are nonetheless certain areas where you could learn from us.'

He struggled against a strong desire to tell her where to put herself.

'I do appreciate,' said Willow, 'that just at this moment you must be feeling antagonistic; that is only to be expected. But later, when you have had a chance to reflect, I'm hoping you may see us in a rather different light. For if we could be said to have learnt our lesson rather too well, it does strike me,' said Willow, 'from the sound of things, that you have learnt no lesson at all.' She smiled at him. 'Think on it,' she said.

Patronising. Patronising! Always so damned *patronising*.

'You see, miss?' Fortune clawed at April's shoulder as they made their way from the crowded hall. 'You see what you've brought on us?'

April shrugged her off, impatiently. She had more important things to do than exchange unpleasantries with Fortune. Wittering old ninny.

'Your mother – ' began Fortune.

April saw a space between two people and dived through it. Somewhere to her right she caught a glimpse of Meta, but she didn't want to talk to Meta just at this moment. Meta had behaved disgracefully. She had betrayed a confidence – well, not a confidence exactly, but to take something which April had told her in private and use it against Daniel, in public, before the whole community, was shameful and unworthy.

David was another who had betrayed her, and even more woundingly than Meta. He had revived childhood memories, re-awoken the friendship that once they had had, engaged her emotions and flung them back in her face. She didn't want to talk to David, either.

She elbowed her way past him (she had just time to see the hurt look on his face. What had *he* got to be hurt about?) shot out through the doors and across the courtyard to the hospital wing. Willow's office was empty; she must still be in with Daniel.

Determinedly April set off up the corridor. She didn't see why she shouldn't; there was no one to stop her. And anyway, she didn't care any more.

'April!' Willow had just come out of Daniel's room as April turned the corner. 'Can I be of help to you?'

'I need to talk to you,' said April.

'Immediately?'

'Before Daniel leaves.'

'He's leaving in the morning. You can come and say goodbye to him – I would have told you. We shall be at the horse field at dawn.'

Willow nodded, amiably, and made to walk on, plainly expecting April to walk with her.

Plainly expecting that that was an end of it.

'I want to do more than just say goodbye to him.' April announced it, breathlessly. 'I want to go with him.'

Willow stiffened. Her face froze and became a mask.

'You had better come into the office,' she said.

April would have preferred to discuss it in front of Daniel, but Willow, already, was headed back up the corridor, not even troubling to turn her head and check that April was following. She took it for granted that she would. It occurred to April that Willow and some of the others took rather a lot for granted.

'Now, then.' Willow drew up a chair. 'Sit down and let's talk this out. You realise, of course, that what you're proposing is not possible?'

April's chin jerked up. 'Why not?'

The mask hardened. Willow was not accustomed to have sixteen-year-olds defy her.

'Simply and plainly, April, because we need you. Is that not reason enough?'

April set her lips. She hadn't quite the courage to say an outright *no*, but she certainly wasn't going to be browbeaten into saying yes.

'Explain to me,' said Willow, 'why you think you want to go with him?'

I don't *think*, thought April; I *know*.

'Does his community really sound so attractive? People carrying firearms? Slaughtering living creatures? Slaughtering each *other*? Men dictating to women what they can and cannot do? Is that really the sort of society you want to live in?'

'N-no, n-not exactly, but – I might be able to help change it!'

'I doubt that, child. Not in your lifetime.'

186

'Well, but if I stayed here I couldn't change anything here, either, could I?'

Willow considered her a moment. 'You think that things need changing here?'

'Yes! I do! I agree with David. I think after all this time we ought to have learnt how to deal with male aggression and not let men push us around and tell us what to do.'

'I'm not sure how you think we should have learnt to deal with it,' murmured Willow, 'when for the last hundred years we have had no experience of it.'

'No, but we've learnt how to be assertive and get things done. And I can't imagine,' said April, daring for a moment to be a bit cheeky, 'I can't imagine you or Rowan ever letting men dictate to you!'

The corner of Willow's mouth lifted just slightly.

'Rowan and I, maybe not. But how about you? You honestly believe, if you go off with Daniel, that you won't be subject to the same rules as the rest of the women?' She shook her head. 'Believe me, it would be disastrous! You would either end up as little better than a chattel, with your spirit broken, or in a state of permanent rebellion – and consequent isolation.'

'Just like David's going to!'

'Because he spoke his mind?'

'He didn't get much support,' said April, 'did he?'

'So why not stay and lend him yours? Instead of running away from the problem, why not stay and try to solve it?'

'Because it isn't going to be solved! Because you're not going to let it!'

'How do you know until you've tried?'

'I don't want to try!' David had betrayed her just as much as Meta. He had forfeited all right to her support. 'I want to get out of here, I want to see other people, I want to see other places, I want to explore!'

'I'm sure we could find other brave souls to explore with you, if that's what you really want. There's no law that says you have to stay confined for the rest of your life. But that's very different from cutting yourself off from everything you know and going to live in an alien community whose ways, I promise you, you would find most abhorrent.'

Willow didn't understand. There wasn't anything here for her any more. She had lost Meta – or they had lost each other; David had done something for which she could never forgive him. There was nothing here to keep her.

'April, I'm sorry,' said Willow. 'The answer has to be no.'

'You mean – ' She was almost too stunned to put the question. It went against everything she had been brought up to believe – 'you mean you would actually stop me?'

'*I* wouldn't stop you,' said Willow. 'It would be a community decision. They would be the ones who stopped you – if they felt as I did, that is. I shouldn't make assumptions on their behalf. Put it to them, ask them, see what they say.'

'You know what they'd say!' *Your mother would turn in her grave* ... 'They're all so *blinkered*!'

'Then it would be up to you to unblinker them. If you think you have a case, put it to them.'

Resentfully April said, 'They'd never listen to me!'

'Of course they would listen.'

'Yes, and say just the same as you've said! The answer has to be *no* ... at least Daniel's community didn't say that.'

'Daniel wasn't proposing to leave for good. And I would remind you that they did say it to his sister.'

'So where is the difference,' said April, 'between them saying no to his sister and you saying no to me?'

'Our reasons are different. We believe that you are of too great a value to the community to be spared: they believe that the activities of females should be restricted simply because they are females.'

'Just like we believe that the activities of men should be restricted simply because they are men!'

There was a pause.

'Yes,' said Willow. 'That is so.'

'If David wanted to go, would you let him?'

'He would have to put it to the community, just as you would.'

'But what would they say? They'd say yes, wouldn't they? Because who needs men? Once they've fulfilled their biological function they're no more use to us, are they? Once you've taken what you want –'

'That is putting it rather crudely, but – yes; broadly speaking you are right.'

'So the only reason I have to stay is that I haven't yet fulfilled my function? If that's the case,' cried April, 'it makes us little better than *breeding* machines!'

The colour drained from Willow's cheeks.

'That is a very terrible thing to say, April. You know as well as I that no one is forced to bear a child against her will.'

'So if I have the choice and I decide not to, what is the point of my staying? I'm no more use to you than David!'

'I wasn't aware that you had decided not to.'

'Well, I have! I wouldn't do anything to help a community that holds people against their will!'

A long silence fell. April felt herself shaking. She had done battle with Willow and still couldn't be sure whether the final shots had been fired or whether she was about to be annihilated.

'Very well.' Willow spoke heavily. 'I can't really answer that, can I? You've made your point; I accept it. Of course we wouldn't dream of holding you against your will. If you feel so strongly about it, then you had better pack what things you wish to take and be ready to leave with Daniel first thing in the morning. But don't, I beg you, whatever you do, feel too proud to admit it if you have a change of heart. We can ill afford to lose any of the community, least of all someone with your spirit. We need people like you to keep us on our toes – we need people to jolt us out of our complacency every now and again, make us question our assumptions. I very much don't want to see you go, April – but if you insist, then so be it.'

Grateful colour flooded April's cheeks.

'It needn't be for ever!' she said. 'I could always come back and visit.'

'I don't somehow think you would find it that easy. I doubt they would allow you. Sleep on it – talk to Meta. Try to be very sure you know what you are doing.'

She did know what she was doing; she was very sure. And there was no point in sleeping on it because she wasn't the sort who slept on things. Like Harriet before her, she preferred to act on impulse. As for talking to Meta, that was out of the question. She and Meta had nothing more to say to each other.

On leaving Willow's office she bumped into David, going about his business. She thought at first that he wasn't going to speak to her. She thought, 'That suits me,' still hurt as she was, and cross, too, but at the last minute he turned and said, 'Thank you for your support.'

Stupidly she said, 'What support?'

'Exactly,' said David. 'What support?'

'You expect me to support you?' she cried. 'After what you did?'

'What do you mean, after what I did?'

'Telling Willow —' She choked.

'Telling Willow what?'

'You know very well what!'

'If you're referring to your clandestine visits —'

'You were the only one who knew about them!'

'Oh, was I? If I were you,' said David, 'I should try looking a little closer to home!'

He turned and strode on, down the corridor. Furiously she ran after him.

'What do you mean? Who are you talking about?'

'Who do you think I'm talking about?'

'*Meta*?'

'She's about as close to home as you can get, isn't she?'

There was a stunned silence. She stared at him, disbelieving — yet knowing, at the same time, it was the truth.

'Well! Thank you not only for your support,' said David, 'but also for your vote of confidence. You obviously have deep faith in me.'

'David, I –'

She caught at his sleeve: he shook her off.

'I hadn't realised you held me in quite such contempt.'

Slowly, April walked back down the road to the girls' house. Holly and Dell were coming towards her. They were hand in hand, a fact she scarcely registered at the time. Holly said, 'You'd better bunnyhop it upstairs right away if you want to hang on to your property.'

April gazed at her, blankly. 'What property?'

'Well, I'm not talking about the contents of your wardrobe,' said Holly.

'You want to get up there toot sweet,' said Dell.

There was nothing more pathetic than Holly and Dell when they were trying to be cryptic. April trailed up the stairs, not relishing what lay ahead, whatever it might be. To her surprise, she found Meta busily stuffing clothes into a bag.

'What are you doing?' she said.

'Moving out,' said Meta. She straightened up, tried to look April in the eye and couldn't quite manage it. She turned, and snatched at a pair of shoes. 'I'm going to share with Linden.'

'Linden? But what about Holly?'

'Holly's gone in with Dell.' Meta crammed the shoes down the side of the bag. 'I know I should have discussed it with you but you haven't ever seemed to be around ... too busy climbing through windows to see your Neanderthal boyfriend.'

April sank down on her bed.

'How did you know?'

'I didn't; I guessed. That night you said you were late because you'd been talking to David –'

Meta pushed her hair behind her ears. 'I knew you couldn't have been, because David was with Willow. And then you kept having headaches and making excuses not to do things. And then you told me about his brother being killed, and how could you have known about his brother being killed if you hadn't been talking to him? If you'd known about it before you'd have told me before. So then I – I followed you, if you want to know.'

'And then you went and used it against him!'

'Well, why shouldn't I?' said Meta. 'It wasn't supposed to be a secret, was it?'

'It was taking a mean advantage!'

'Yes, well, you were taking a mean advantage! Doing things behind my back – having *secrets* – ' Meta choked. 'How would you have felt if I'd done that to you?'

'Meta, I'm sorry!' April sprang up, impulsively, from the bed. 'I'm sorry! I didn't mean it!'

'You might at least have told me.'

'I know, I know, but I didn't want us having a row!'

'What does a row matter? Anything's better than deceiving each other. If a relationship can't stand up to the truth, then what sort of relationship is it? Anyway – ' agitatedly, Meta twisted a length of scarf round her hand – 'it doesn't matter any more.'

No, it doesn't, thought April. This time tomorrow she would be – where? In London? – with Daniel. She should have felt elated; instead, a deep melancholy settled on her.

'I'm sorry, too,' said Meta. 'It's horrid it should end this way, but – Holly and Lin had already broken up, and Lin and I – '

April said quickly, 'You don't have to explain. I'm glad you've got Linden. She'll be much better for you than I was.'

'But we did have some good times together,' said Meta, anxiously, 'didn't we?'

'I suppose . . . except that I was always making you do things you didn't want to do, like climbing up trees and going on adventures . . . you won't have any of that with Linden. You can be as studious as you like and bore each other silly!'

'Oh, April –'

They clung to each other.

'You'll find someone else soon!' whispered Meta. 'I know you will.'

That made her feel guilty. She prised herself away.

'I hope you and Linden will be very happy,' she said. 'I think you're absolutely right for each other, and – whatever happens, please don't think too badly of me.'

Meta looked at her, suddenly suspicious. 'You're not going to do anything foolish?'

'Go away!' April gave her a push. 'You're not allowed to bully me any more!'

'Me bully *you*?' said Meta. 'I like that!'

They spent the last few minutes fooling around and joking. April was glad, at least, that they weren't ending in bitterness and recrimination, but it came upon her yet again how much she was going to miss Meta. You couldn't be intimate with someone for sixteen years and cut yourself off with no regrets, however exciting and different your new life was going to be.

A great loneliness swamped her when she was finally left on her own. Meta was only moving up to the next floor, yet it seemed a world away. Hastily she threw open a drawer and began rifling through its contents, trying to concentrate her mind on what she needed to take with her. She ought to have told Meta, she knew that, but she had been terrified of spoiling their last few precious minutes together. She couldn't bear to leave with bad memories.

A knock came at the door. She went to open it and found David standing there.

'I just bumped into Holly,' he said.

'Oh! Yes. Holly.'

'Yes.'

There was a pause; awkward on both sides.

'I'm really sorry – ' began April, as the same time as David said, 'She told me –'

They stopped.

'After you,' said David.

'I'm really sorry I thought it was you who told Willow about me and Daniel.'

'That's all right. It was probably a natural enough conclusion . . . in the circumstances.'

'I am sorry, though.'

'It doesn't matter.'

'So what were you –'

'About Holly.'

'Yes.'

'She told me that – that you and Meta were splitting up.'

'Meta's moving in with Linden.'

'Yes.' David wiped the back of his thumb across his forehead. 'I was wondering if you – if you haven't made any other plans, that is – if you'd care to . . . move in with me.'

That suggestion took her by surprise. It was the last thing she had expected.

'It has been known,' said David. 'I mean . . .

we wouldn't be the first.'

'It's not that,' burst out April, 'it's just that I – I'm going with Daniel!'

'Oh.' Two spots of colour burned in David's cheeks. 'I guess I shouldn't have asked you. That was stupid of me.'

'It wasn't stupid. It was nice of you, and I would have said yes if – '

'If something better hadn't turned up. It's all right, you don't have to apologise, I understand. When are you leaving?'

'Tomorrow morning. Very early.'

'Am I allowed to come and say goodbye? Or would you rather I didn't?'

She hesitated.

'You'd rather I didn't.'

'It's j – '

'I told you, don't apologise!'

'B – '

'April.' He took both her hands in his. 'If this is what you want, then I'm very happy for you. I just hope,' he said, 'that you know what you're doing!'

He was off down the stairs before she could say anything. She leaned out, over the banisters.

'David – '

He halted in mid-flight to look up at her.

'Good luck!' called April.

She was up with the dawn. She had no difficulty waking: she hadn't been to sleep, but had sat all night by the open window, watching the sky and wondering.

All kinds of things she had wondered about. The new life she was going to, the old life she was leaving . . . Would Meta miss her, when she

196

was no longer there? Would she and Linden stay together, through the years? Would they end up a force in the community, like Rowan and Willow? April would never know. And David... what of David? Would he go on fighting his lone battle? How would he manage, without April to support him? Would he lose heart and give up, or stand firm and find himself ostracised? John and Delian and their cronies, Linnet and Fortune and all those who claimed to have memories, they would all be against him. Rowan and Willow would listen, they would give him a fair hearing, but still he would be on his own; and nothing would change. How long could a person carry on without encouragement?

A picture came to her of David in ten, twenty years' time, worn out with the struggle, giving way to the forces ranged against him, sad and grey and defeated. It upset her, to think of David like that. Suppose she were to ask Daniel if he could come with them? Would he want to? Or would he consider that to be running away? It was so hard to decide where loyalties should lie: with oneself or with one's community?

Drifting thus, in and out of her thoughts, April had passed the night.

Now she crept downstairs, carrying just one large bag full of clothes, plus one or two of her personal possessions – pencil drawings of her mother and Meta, some odds and ends of jewellery which she had found on scavving expeditions and been allowed to keep, a story she and Meta had written together at the age of eleven, about two girls who 'rode off down the valley in search of adventure'. Whether they had found it or not the reader had never been permitted to know, for Meta had decreed that all the best stories 'left people guessing'.

April let herself quietly out of the front door and turned right, away from the Hall and towards the fields where she must meet Daniel. She reached the lane with its faded signpost pointing the way to a church which had long since crumbled and gone. There for a moment she hesitated; then somewhere in the distance a horse whinnied and she gave a little sigh, shifted her bag from one hand to the other and continued on her way.

As she set off down the lane a black shape appeared, hurtling joyously towards her.

'Shep!' she cried.

She kneaded his ruff and he leapt at her, paws on shoulders, tongue washing her face, before turning and bounding confidently down the lane ahead of her, plume high, in full expectation of adventure.

April followed, more slowly, until they came at last to the field where the horses were kept. Shep cleared the gate in one easy bound, ran a few yards, turned and crouched, waiting for her to open the gate and let herself in.

Across the field, in the early morning light, she could see Willow and Daniel putting a bridle on one of the horses. She waited a while, watching them. A movement suddenly caught her eye. She turned her head, sharply, in time to glimpse a shadow disappearing into the hedge.

'David?' she said.

He stepped out, shamefaced, into the lane.

'I wasn't spying on you!'

April laughed, a little shakily. 'You s-said that once before.'

'Did I? Yes, so I did. You must think I'm some

kind of pervert, always skulking in dark corners. I just – I just felt – after all this time – I couldn't – not come and – say a proper goodbye. I – look, I won't hang around. Forgive me. I – ' He bent, quickly, and brushed his lips against hers. 'I hope you'll be very happy!'

He turned, to go back up the lane.

'David!' She sprang after him. 'Wait just a second. Hold this for me – ' She thrust her bag at him. 'I won't be a minute.'

David watched as she walked through into the field. He saw two figures come towards her, one of them leading a horse. As they drew nearer, he recognised the one leading the horse as Daniel. They stopped as April reached them. He heard the low murmur of voices, then Willow took the bridle and urged the horse on towards the gate, leaving Daniel and April together.

David turned away. He felt that he had seen enough. He ought never to have come.

After a bit, he heard a creak as the gate was swung open. He set April's bag in the middle of the path and shrank back into the hedge. A horse trotted out of the field with a lone rider. At the sight of the bag it shied, but the rider sat tight. He raised a hand in salute as he passed.

'You win,' he said, simply.

David spun round, to see April closing the gate behind her and Willow.

'April?' he said. 'What's happening?'

'Nothing's happening. I changed my mind, that's all.' April slipped her hand into his, squeezing it hard. 'I promised I'd give you my support, didn't I?'

He stiffened. 'You don't have to stay on my account.'

'Why not?' she said. 'If that's what I want?'

He looked at her, gravely. 'Is it what you want?'

Behind them, Willow said, 'You ought to know by now, David, that April never does anything she doesn't choose to do.'

'Exactly,' said April.

Willow walked briskly past them, Shep following at her heels.

'I can see we're going to have trouble on our hands with you two.'

David grinned, as he picked up April's bag. 'I hope so,' he said. 'I certainly hope so . . .'

Jean Ure

WATCHERS AT THE SHRINE

'Hal, if you stay on here, you know perfectly well what will happen to you.'

'Yes! The same as'll happen to all the others. Why do I have to be different?'

Hal's mother April has his best interests at heart when she and David send him away from the Croydon Community to avoid ritual castration. But now Hal is an outcast from his own community and is sent to live in Cornishtown, where the aggressive ways of the twentieth century survive 150 years after the plague struck.

Hal has to live with a family of Watchers, out-dwellers with a religion that demands absolute obedience to the Power. On a journey to the shrine, Hal discovers a terrible truth – but where can he go to be safe?

This is the fascinating conclusion to the 'Plague' trilogy, begun in *Plague* and continued in *After the Plague* (originally published as *Come Lucky April*).